FOREST OF SECRETS

ALEXIS FORREST MYSTERY
BOOK 3

KATE GABLE

KATE GABLE

COPYRIGHT

Visit my website at www.kategable.com

BE THE FIRST TO KNOW ABOUT MY UPCOMING SALES, NEW RELEASES AND EXCLUSIVE GIVEAWAYS!

W ant a Free book? Sign up for my Newsletter!

Sign up for my newsletter:
https://www.subscribepage.com/kategableviplist

Join my Facebook Group:
https://www.facebook.com/groups/
833851020557518

Bonus Points: Follow me on BookBub and
Goodreads!

https://www.goodreads.com/author/show/21534224.
Kate_Gable

ABOUT KATE GABLE

Kate Gable is a 3 time Silke Falchion award winner including Book of the Year. She loves a good mystery that is full of suspense. She grew up devouring psychological thrillers and crime novels as well as movies, tv shows and true crime.

Her favorite stories are the ones that are centered on families with lots of secrets and lies as well as many twists and turns. Her novels have elements of psychological suspense, thriller, mystery and romance.

Kate Gable lives near Palm Springs, CA with her husband, son, a dog and a cat. She has spent more than twenty years in Southern California and finds inspiration from its cities, canyons, deserts, and small mountain towns.

She graduated from University of Southern California with a Bachelor's degree in Mathematics. After pursuing graduate studies in mathematics, she switched gears and got her MA in Creative Writing and English from Western New Mexico University and her PhD in Education from Old Dominion University.

Writing has always been her passion and obsession. Kate is also a USA Today Bestselling author of romantic suspense under another pen name.

Write her here:

Kate@kategable.com

Check out her books here:

www.kategable.com

Sign up for my newsletter:
https://www.subscribepage.com/kategableviplist

Join my Facebook Group:
https://www.facebook.com/groups/
833851020557518

Bonus Points: Follow me on BookBub and Goodreads!

https://www.bookbub.com/authors/kate-gable

https://www.goodreads.com/author/show/21534224.
Kate_Gable

ALSO BY KATE GABLE

Detective Kaitlyn Carr Psychological Mystery series
Girl Missing (Book 1)
Girl Lost (Book 2)
Girl Found (Book 3)
Girl Taken (Book 4)
Girl Forgotten (Book 5)
Gone Too Soon (Book 6)
Gone Forever (Book 7)
Whispers in the Sand (Book 8)

Girl Hidden (FREE Novella)

Detective Charlotte Pierce Psychological Mystery series
Last Breath
Nameless Girl

Missing Lives
Girl in the Lake

ABOUT FOREST OF SECRETS

Forensic psychologist and FBI agent Alexis Forrest's search for the serial killer responsible for her sister's murder has hit a wall. All the evidence she has found has led her to the identities of numerous victims, yet the killer is still unknown.

But he knows who she is, and he is watching her from the shadows. He is hiding in plain sight near Broken Hill, the snowy New England town that Alexis used to call home.

Meanwhile, a young suburban mother goes missing while out on a morning run. When Alexis starts to dig deeper, she finds out that the woman's perfect marriage and family are not what they seem. Secrets and resentments are swirling around the couple. Did someone take her or was it the husband after all?

While Alexis is busy with her new case, the serial killer continues to watch. He is close. Close enough to strike.

Can Alexis find the woman before she's killed? Can she figure out who is stalking her before he makes his move?

1

ALYSSA

How was it that no matter how well she prepared the night before, no matter how careful she was to have everything in place, mornings were always a total sprint to the finish line?

"Come on, you two." Alyssa cleared away the breakfast dishes and left them in the sink. "Hannah, please finish your juice. Dylan, why did you take your shoes off?" It wasn't easy to keep her voice calm when she made such a discovery.

"My feet are sweaty!" As if to prove his point, her three-year-old son stuck out one of his feet and wiggled his sock-covered toes. "I need to wiggle!"

"I know you need to wiggle, but you also need to wear shoes if we're going to leave the house. It's cold out there." At least he wasn't taking the rest of his clothes off. Funny how low the bar could sink when it came to raising kids.

"Oh, no!" Hannah looked down at her sweater, which was now covered in orange juice. She had coughed while gulping what was left in her cup, and the result made Alyssa's head pound.

"It's alright," she murmured when Hannah's eyes filled with tears. "We'll take care of it."

Then, turning away, she called out to her husband. "Connor? Please bring down another sweater for Hannah. We had an accident."

"But it's Pink Day!" Hannah groaned. "We're all supposed to wear pink!

"Find something pink?" Alyssa added, raising her voice to be heard upstairs. "It can be a sweatshirt or a turtleneck, whatever."

"But I want to wear this sweater!" Tears spilled onto Hannah's chubby cheeks, and Alyssa reminded herself that four-year-olds felt things more acutely than older kids. And a smart, responsible little girl like Hannah felt them even more intensely. She was conscientious to a fault, much like her mother.

"I know, honey. But there's just no time to clean it. You have so many beautiful clothes." There was nothing Alyssa could say to make things better, so she settled for a tight hug after pulling the wet, sticky sweater over her daughter's head. "It's okay. It's going to be okay."

"I heard somebody is in need of a pink shirt." Connor strode into the room, and instantly the tension popped like an overinflated balloon. Somehow, he always found a way to make things better simply by existing. It had always been that way, and his level-headed calmness was one of the qualities that had first attracted her to him. After a childhood spent in the presence of parents who fought like cats and dogs–on a good day–Connor was her refuge.

"I spilled, Daddy." Hannah's bottom lip stuck out in a pout.

"It happens to the best of us. Heck, I spill things all the time." He went about helping Hannah get into her new sweatshirt while Alyssa replaced Dylan's shoes in spite of his protests.

"You do?" The tiniest bit of hope entered Hannah's voice.

"Almost every day. Mommy will tell you. I'm a total klutz."

"He is," Alyssa agreed, then gave him a quick kiss in passing.

"Mommy called Daddy a klutz!" Dylan found this extremely funny. "Klutz, klutz, klutz!"

"You even know what that means?" Hannah asked.

"Nope!" But that did nothing to lessen his enjoyment. Alyssa glanced at her husband and bit her lip, fighting to stifle a laugh.

"I hope that's not all you plan on having for breakfast." She eyed the travel cup of coffee Connor filled at the kitchen counter.

"I'm already running late." He checked his watch, scowling. "Meredith's going to bring in bagels and muffins today, anyway."

"I wish I had an assistant to bring me breakfast."

Connor chuckled before pressing a quick kiss to her cheek in passing. "Just wait. Once everything is settled with the practice, you can hire all the help you want. You wouldn't have to lift a finger around here. You could even go back to work, if you wanted to."

"One thing at a time." Because it was nice to think about things like that, very nice, but it was also better to control her expectations. Connor was a good husband, and a good provider, but he also had a tendency to leap before looking. Not that starting his own dermatology practice with his partner was a bad idea – she would never have held him back. But building a business involved the same level of hard work and patience no matter what a person did for a living. This would not be an overnight success.

"Let's go!" She clapped her hands briskly, grabbing the kids' backpacks from where she had left them by the front door before going to bed. "We don't want to be late."

"You heard your mother." Connor helped Hannah into her coat while she managed to get Dylan into his. Some days, it was like herding cats. Today was one of those days.

"Hold your sleeve," she murmured, tucking it into his little fist before sliding the coat over top. "See? And now it didn't get all bunched up."

"You're so smart, Mommy." It didn't take much to impress a three-year-old, but her son's sweet words and the sincerity that rang out in them warmed her heart. Yes, there were times when she missed the hustle and bustle of her old career. She missed business trips and weekend brunches and getting together for drinks with the girls after work. She missed feeling … respected. Not that Connor disrespected her, but it was a different sort of respect. She was a good wife, but excellent homemaker, a great cook. And he respected that. But he used to respect her smarts, her savvy. Where had that gone?

"As hectic as this was," she told him on their way out the door, "you made it easier."

"That's what I'm here for." They exchanged a quick but meaningful look before kissing briefly, chuckling over the way the kids groaned. Even at their young age, they thought it was icky for their parents to show affection. It would only get worse the older they got.

She hustled the kids out the door and into their car seats, and they waved in unison when Connor backed out of his spot and tapped the horn. "Is Daddy going to work late tonight?" Hannah asked, craning her neck to follow the car's progress.

"He said he wouldn't. He'll be home for dinner."

"Really?" Dylan's eyes went round. "Daddy will have dinner with us? But it's not even the weekend!"

This was what she had tried to explain to Connor. The kids were too young to understand why he was absent so much of the time. They might understand someday, but by then, the damage would be done. They would grow up while he was in the office, and by the time things settled down and he had more time to spend, he would've already missed so much – and they might not be quite so willing to open up and let him into their little worlds. Not out of spite, but out of habit. She knew all too well how that felt.

"You said we were going to be late!"

Hannah's plaintive cry snapped Alyssa out of her reverie. She narrowed her eyes at her daughter in the rearview mirror. "Okay, Little Miss. Thanks for keeping Mom on track."

On the way to the preschool, roughly fifteen minutes from the house, they listened to a kids channel on the satellite radio. The drive to school turned into a concert, with Hannah warbling her way through every song, even if she didn't quite remember the lyrics. Dylan was happy simply to clap along, always enthusiastic. If only they would always stay so small, so trusting and innocent. So eager to live and laugh and feel joy. But every day they got a little older, a little wiser. Hopefully, it would be a long time before they became jaded.

"Here we are!" Alyssa waved to a couple of the other moms as she pulled into the lot alongside the preschool. As usual, Hannah tried to call out to her friends when she spotted them, and Alyssa had to explain yet again that it wasn't easy to hear her voice with the windows rolled up. "You'll have plenty of time to talk to Molly and Sadie when you get inside," she reminded her daughter after helping her from her car seat.

"Why do girls have to yell so much?" Dylan wondered aloud. "You're always yelling and always talking."

"And you are too young to be so cynical," Alyssa laughed, kissing his cheek before helping him jump from the car onto the pavement. She walked with them to the front doors, then waved goodbye. As usual, Hannah took Dylan's hand, ready to lead him to his classroom before going to her own. It was moments like that which made everything worthwhile. Watching her children love each other. The time might come when they would fight like cats and dogs – she was under no illusions. For the time being, though, this was nice.

"Lyss! We're going to Starbies. Wanna come?" Sadie's mother, Elizabeth, waved while wearing a friendly smile, standing beside her Mercedes.

Alyssa shook her head, though. "The kitchen is a mess, and I want to get my run in. Next time."

"I wish we all had your discipline." Alyssa only laughed and waved goodbye before heading back to her SUV. Discipline was only half the story. The other half? It had already been a long morning and she didn't have the energy to gossip with the girls. Sometimes, it was better for her peace of mind to be on her own.

The first thing she did when she returned to the driver seat, switch the station to something more her style. An early Madonna tune soon filled the car, and she sang along, fingers tapping the wheel in time with the happy, upbeat song. The next song was by Journey, and she belted her lungs out before Culture Club's Karma Chameleon left her bouncing in her seat.

The ride passed in the blink of an eye, and she was grinning from ear to ear by the time she pulled into her driveway. As usual, the sight of the family's three-thousand square-foot home filled her with a sense of pride. It was the sort of home she'd always dreamed of, somewhere anyone would be proud to call their own.

She hopped out of the car, humming to herself, and headed straight inside to where her running clothes were left in a neat pile on the stairs. There was no way of ignoring them, which was precisely why she'd left them in that spot. She quickly changed and put on her running shoes, then grabbed her AirPods from the table beside the door and pulled up her running playlist before sliding her phone into the pocket of her leggings. It was a little slippery out there, but she didn't want to skip the run.

Some days, running was all that kept her together.

She went outside, careful to lock the door behind her, then stretched on the porch before jogging down the driveway. The garland was waiting to be hung in swags from the porch roof, but that could wait. It had been too long since she'd gone out of her way to put herself first.

2

CONNOR

"And what about these?" The woman in the chair touched her fingertips to the crow's feet at the outer corners of both eyes. Anxiety rang clear in her voice. "Can you smooth these out?"

"Of course. That's what we do. And they're still in the early stages," Connor mused, examining the patient's skin up-close. Danica Andrews was the sort of woman who must have been a stunner in her day but, as was so often the case, time had begun catching up with her. Patients like this were his bread and butter, the very thing that kept the dermatology practice running. The quest to maintain youth in beauty was what put food on the table and kept the kids in a pretty pricey school.

"We can certainly add treatment of these little guys to your regular Botox injection. Otherwise, though, the cleanser and moisturizer I recommended during your last visit seems to be working just fine. Have you noticed the difference in your skin's elasticity?"

"Oh, definitely, and it's not nearly as red or sensitive."

"That's good to hear. We're on the right track."

A quick knock at the door to the exam room preceded the door opening a crack so Meredith could poke her head into the room. "Excuse me, Dr. Lawrence, but there's a call for you."

"I'm with a patient," he reminded her in a light but firm voice.

She winced but stayed in place. "It's from the kids' school. They're still waiting to be picked up."

Right away, he sought the clock hanging over the door. It was a quarter past three – not only had the day melted away, but the kids should have been picked up fifteen minutes ago.

"Excuse me," he murmured, standing and removing his mask and gloves. "I'll be right back." He went no further than the phone mounted on the wall outside the exam room and hit the blinking button. "This is Connor Lawrence. What's the matter? Are the kids alright?"

"The children are fine, but your wife hasn't yet arrived for pick-up, and we can't reach her on her cell."

Fifteen minutes. If this were anyone else, fifteen minutes might not seem like a matter of any urgency. Fifteen minutes could mean getting stuck behind a bus or miscalculating the amount of time it took to run an errand.

But not Alyssa. And even if she were late, she would have called the school to let them know.

"Alright. I'll be there as soon as I can to grab the kids. Let them know I'm on my way." After hanging up, he pulled his cell from his back pocket. There were no missed calls or texts from his wife, nothing to indicate trouble. He placed a call to her before striding down the hall toward his partner's office, but there was no answer.

"Dr. Chett?" Connor tapped on the door before opening it to reveal his partner, the man who'd mentored him for years. The twenty-year gap in their ages may have seemed on paper to make them an unlikely duo, but nothing could've been further from the truth. Samuel Chett possessed the gravitas and experience patients counted on, while Connor was the young, charming, energetic half of their practice.

Samuel looked up from his screen, frowning. "What is it? You look worried."

"I have Danica Andrews in exam room one. Can you please wrap up with her? Routine Botox, all the information is in her file. I'm going to have Meredith reschedule the rest of the afternoon."

"What's wrong?"

"Alyssa never picked up the kids, and I can't reach her on her phone. I have to go grab them, and … figure out what's wrong."

"That's unusual for her." While they weren't exactly close friends, both had brought their spouses for dinner at the other's home numerous times over the years. Samuel had never refrained from expressing admiration at Alyssa's cooking and how easy she made everything look.

"Yeah, no kidding." The men exchanged a look of concern before Connor retreated to his own office at the opposite end of the hall, where he grabbed his things and headed up front. Meredith seemed concerned when he asked her to clear his schedule for the rest of the day, but didn't waste time asking questions. Not that he had the time to answer them.

What could've happened? Was she sick? Maybe she had fallen somewhere in the house. She had talked about getting decorations from the attic. He asked her to wait until he could help her with them, to which she had gently rolled her eyes and reminded him how rarely he was home before nine o'clock anymore. She had always been fiercely independent. That was one of the reasons he fell in love with her. Had that independence reared up to bite her?

The kids were waiting for him in the front office, and he went out of his way to seem cheerful as he crouched to give them both a big hug and apologize for keeping them waiting. "How come you're picking us up?" Dylan asked.

"Because it's a special treat kind of day." He took their bags and thanked the teachers for keeping an eye on the kids before shooing them out the door.

"Did you take the day off?" Hannah asked.

"Something like that."

"Where is Mommy?"

The lump in his throat nearly kept him from answering his daughter's question. "Mommy got stuck running errands, but it's fine. We get to spend a little more time together today." And all the while, an entire range of ugly scenarios ran through his head. What would they walk into once they entered the house? If she were sick or injured, he didn't want the kids to see. Neither would Alyssa.

Apprehension threatened to freeze him in place once he pulled in beside his wife's matching SUV.

Nothing seemed out of the ordinary so far – the front door was closed, everything looked peaceful. The kids rambled on while he got them out of their car seats. He let them go as far as the front porch before crouching in front of them. "I need you to do me a favor, okay? I need you both to wait right here while I go inside."

"How come?" Hannah took Dylan's hand. She'd always been too smart and intuitive. She had to sense something was off.

"Because … Mommy has been working on a surprise for you two for Christmas."

Dylan's mouth fell open. "But that's not for a million years!"

"Closer than that," Connor told him. "I want to be sure she didn't leave it laying around where you can find it. Can you be really good and stay here for just one minute?" The two of them nodded, eyes wide, and he wasted no time unlocking the door and entering the house with his heart in his throat.

"Lyss?" He quickly surveyed the first floor, jogging from room to room. Right away, the sight of plates and cups exactly where they'd been left that morning turned his apprehension to cold, clawing fear. She would never have left things lying around – she always loaded the dishwasher after dropping the kids off.

He dashed up the stairs, calling her name again, but there was hardly a sign of her entering the house after they'd all left together. The bedroom was exactly how he'd left it before heading downstairs, which he did again, this time noticing what he'd missed at first; Alyssa's purse sitting on the table inside the front door. The running shoes she kept on a rack beneath it were missing, and the flats she'd worn that morning sat in their place. She had gone for a run. Her phone wasn't in her purse, either.

Finally, he turned to the only other tool at his disposal, the footage from the doorbell camera. He pulled up the app on his phone and rolled the footage back to earlier in the day, around the time Alyssa would normally be home after drop-off. There she was, leaving on her run, stretching with her AirPods in her ears. Then she jogged down the driveway, taking a left turn at the end and running out of sight.

And as far as he could tell, she never came back.

His hands shook when he joined the kids on the porch, forcing him to jam them into his coat pockets. "You know what?" he said, looking up and down the street, fighting to keep it together when all he wanted to do was scream. "I'm going to call Miss McKenna across the street and see if you guys can watch TV over there for a little while. Would you like that?"

"She has the best cookies!" Clearly, Dylan was sold on the idea. Connor placed the call and McKenna offered to come over and grab the kids once he explained something was wrong without giving any details.

After that, there was one more task to accomplish. He felt like he was moving through a nightmare as he dialed 911. "Yes, my wife is missing. She never came home from her run this morning. We need to find her. Please, help me."

3

ALEXIS

"**K**nock, knock."

Captain Felch looks up from his desk to find me standing in the doorway, holding a cardboard cup carrier with two steaming lattes balanced inside. "I might not be working an active case in town, but that doesn't mean I can't deliver a little caffeine every once in a while."

The lines in his face deepen when he grins. "You sure know how to make yourself necessary."

"What a nice compliment." I hand him one of the cups before taking the other for myself. "Necessary. I like the sound of that."

"You're in a good mood today," he observes, looking me up and down. "Is this all the result of tracking down Charles Nelson? Or is there something else in the air?"

I like the captain very much and respect him even more, but there are certain aspects of my life he doesn't need to be privy to. It just so happens I'm floating on cloud nine for the first time in forever. Professional matters aside, my life is looking better every day. It's all thanks to Mitch Dutton, my high school boyfriend turned current boyfriend, who happened to brew these lattes for us. "What's not to be happy about? I have a fresh cup of caffeine in front of me, and the temperature outside is actually above freezing for the first time in what feels like forever."

"Yes, it's going all the way up to forty degrees. Practically summer." He flips open the lid and takes a sniff of the fragrant brew before sipping carefully. Releasing a little grunt, he says, "I do need to start paying you for this. As much as I appreciate it, it's too much."

"And like I've already told you, I don't pay for it. I'm certainly not going to charge you."

"How is it you manage to get your hands on free lattes all the time?"

"Maybe I know how to sweet talk the man who makes the drinks."

"Oh, I see. Daylight has begun to glimmer." He takes another sip before grinning. "I'm glad. At least

I know you have something in your life besides your work."

"Don't worry about me."

"That is very easy for you to say. When you have a penchant for putting yourself in danger, it's not so simple."

He settles back in his chair, turning the cup this way and that on the desk. "What's the news? Are you transferring out to Portland?"

I was only sent back to my hometown to investigate the disappearance of a young girl – having found her, there's now the question of what comes next. "I haven't heard anything definite, either way. Until I do, I plan to split my time between here and Portland, if they'll let me. Otherwise …"

A knowing grimace flashes across his weathered face. "Otherwise, you wouldn't be able to keep driving down to see your boyfriend."

"Something like that."

"So it's serious, is it?"

"When did this turn into a chat about my private life?" Has he been chatting with Mom?

"When you revealed the first hint of having one."

"Doesn't everybody?"

"Until now, I seriously wondered."

"Anyway, we'll see. Fingers crossed. I would much rather work out of Broken Hill, since this is where Andrew Flynn's last known whereabouts happened to be." I settle into a chair on the other side of his desk. "I don't know what it is, but I feel like this is where I need to be. Mitch aside."

"I see, so it's Mitch Dutton. I had my suspicions."

"How?" I ask with a laugh. I feel a blush heating my cheeks, though I have nothing to be embarrassed about.

"The coffee cups. I get around, Agent Forrest. I don't live behind my desk." He lifts his cup and points at the stack of books printed along one side. "They're quite distinctive."

"You got me. Yes, it's Mitch. We dated all through high school, so reconnecting like this has been an unexpected bonus."

"Considering how difficult it must have been for you to come back, it's good to know you've had someone to soften the more difficult aspects."

Though he offers his thoughts gently, kindly, that doesn't keep them from stirring sadness in my chest. The sort of sadness that always lives there, having set up camp years ago. It's not the sort of thing a person can get rid of. They can only learn to live with it.

The way I learned to live with my sister's murder. The effects of it still ripple through my life to this day, and those ripples have only turned to small waves over the weeks since I came back to Broken Hill. Finding her picture along with the articles detailing her gruesome death in the cabin of a man wanted for kidnapping and murder threw open the curtains and cast bright, glaring sunlight on the pain and the loss.

"Speaking of which …" He clears his throat and offers an awkward, sheepish little grin at his sudden change in topic. "How is it going? It isn't easy, being out of the loop when it was our department who helped uncover the cabin."

I can only imagine how frantic and frustrated I would be if I couldn't pursue a case I felt so close to. "The Bureau hasn't made any significant progress. I drove out to the field office last week and went through the files. That was what first gave me the idea to visit the Blitzers—I told you I was going to do that, right?" His head bobs. "To think. She had already been gone almost nine years before my sister was kidnapped. I hadn't even been born yet when Crystal was kidnapped, not for another few months."

"If only they had caught him back then." He gives me the sort of look that tells me an awkward question is about to follow. "How are you handling it? Did you ever tell your parents what we found?"

I nod, emotion clogging my throat until I swallow the lump back. "Yes, they know. I wanted to wait until we had more evidence before breaking the news to my dad, but I was afraid someone else would somehow get word that we found Maddie's photo in the cabin. A lot of people around town still remember that."

"Because a lot of people around town remember the shooting that followed."

I still can't help but cringe when I think of my sweet, kind father opening fire on the man convicted of kidnapping and strangling my sister. The story made headlines for a week, then circulated around the country for a while after that. *Grieving Father Takes Justice Into His Own Hands*. That's the kind of story people can't resist.

"I went to see him," I confess.

"Your father?"

"Russell Duffy. My sister's supposed murderer. I visited him in prison."

His mouth falls open before he can contain himself. "Alexis. I had no idea you were going to do that. What happened?"

"He's turned his life around and actually credits going to prison with saving his life. If you can believe it, he even told me to tell Dad he forgives him, and that he understands why he tried to kill him."

A deep sigh puffs out his cheeks. "I can't imagine that was easy to hear. Have you told your father?"

"It hit him hard. I've been checking in, making sure he's alright. He seems to be doing well."

"And did you two discuss Maddie's murder while you were at the prison?"

"Of course, he claims he's innocent."

"They usually do." He pauses, lowering his brow. Here comes another loaded question. "Did you believe him?"

"Yes. I believed him. And not because of the cabin, either. He was very honest about himself. He didn't have any reason to lie. And he didn't strike me as a violent person. Just someone who made a lot of rotten choices that worked against him at the worst possible time."

"That's a terrible thing, imagining he went to prison for someone else's crime. I'm glad he could at least find some good in it." He's already finished his latte, and he tosses the empty cup into the can beneath his desk. "You never did tell me how it went when you visited with the Blitzers."

"According to the timeline established around all the articles and photos, it was Crystal Blitzer who died first. That was all the way back in 1994. She was found a few days after she went missing while walking home from a babysitting job."

"He's an opportunist. He picked Camille Martin up as she was walking home, didn't he?"

"Yes, and he picked up Lila Kirkman when she sneaked over the wall at Hawthorne Academy." It still sticks in my craw, the question of whether or not he offered to help her get away. He was working as a maintenance man at the Academy. Did he happen to find her fleeing by accident, or was it planned in advance? Was he supposed to be her getaway driver? That's the sort of question I won't be able to answer until I have the man in front of me.

I haven't shared the most chilling aspect. "When I described the location of the cabin where Camille was held, the Blitzers recognized it right away. I still have photos from the last vacation they took before Crystal died. It was in the cabin."

"That's pretty significant. How did they take it?"

Susan Blitzer's heartbroken cries echo in my head. "Mrs. Blitzer broke down. It hit them both pretty hard."

"I can only imagine." We exchange a look with plenty of meaning behind it. I can read his thoughts. The family is tied to the cabin. What does that mean? Did they know Andrew Flynn, or whatever his name is?

"Maybe he wasn't going by Andrew Flynn back then," the captain muses. "He could've been going by another name. His real name."

"Here's hoping this is a step in the right direction."

I wonder how many other families are tied to this man.

More importantly, I wonder if my sister was.

4

ALEXIS

"I am really going to miss these." I lick my fork, and press it to my plate to pick up every last buttery crumb left behind by the massive slice of quiche Mitch served up when I met him at the shop for a late lunch. Spinach and feta, my favorite of the varieties he offers.

I glance up from my plate and find his blue eyes troubled, his brows drawn together. And now I realize what I just said without thinking about it. "I'm sorry. It must seem like I'm looking forward to leaving. Like I can't wait to get away."

"That's not what I thought you meant." He shakes his head a little, releasing a soft chuckle before taking another forkful of the impossibly light creation. "It's not easy to hear. That's all. I don't like to think about you leaving."

"I don't like to think about it, either," I admit. "Really."

"I feel like I just got you back. All those years of not seeing you, and then you walk back into my life."

"It was unexpected, for sure." Aside from having a warmer relationship with my mother and reconnecting with Dad, this new relationship with Mitch is the most important aspect of my return. I can't actually say we've gotten back together, because we're different people from the ones we were the day I first left town, heading for college and what I hoped would be a much brighter future than any that would be afforded me if I stuck around here.

I'm sure I made the right decision—I know it in my heart. I couldn't stay. I couldn't marinate for years in grief and shame, couldn't live my life with the specter of my sister's murder and my father's attempted murder of the man who went to prison for the crime hanging over my head. I couldn't let Mom's despair wrap itself around me like a chain attached to an anchor, pulling me down into the darkness where there was no air to breathe. I had to make a life of my own. I needed to be my own person.

It's clear now that I want to be with the man sitting across from me at the small table in the back corner of his café. There are a few customers wandering the bookshop in front, but he only has eyes for me. Not many people get a second chance, but here we are. Now that we re-found each other, I can't walk away.

Sadly, it's not entirely up to me, just like it wasn't up to me to come back in the first place. That, I'm glad of, since I wouldn't have chosen to return. I dreaded it with all my heart when I first got word I would be investigating the Camille Martin case in a town I was sort of hoping I never had to set eyes on again.

Now, I don't want to leave. Funny how life works out.

"Have you heard anything at all about next steps?" he asks.

Shaking my head, I cut myself a small slice of what's left of the quiche. "Of course not. Why in the world would anybody not keep me hanging over this? I hate living in limbo."

"I can't imagine how frustrating that must be for you."

"It can't be easy for you, either," I offer.

"It's not me I'm worried about. It's you. Always you."

"I know." That's another reason I don't want to leave. But even though Portland wouldn't be an unthinkable distance – we could make it work – there's a good chance my request to work the

Andrew Flynn case and dig deeper into his possible crimes could be denied. I could be sent to the other side of the country for all I know.

I lean back in my chair and pat my stomach, blowing out a sigh. "Honestly, maybe it would do my waistline a favor if I went away for a bit. You are no good at helping me keep my diet."

"I wasn't aware you were on one. You don't need it."

"I'm not on a diet, yet, but I'll need one before much longer." We share a quiet laugh, and a delicious shiver runs up my spine when he takes my hand and rubs his thumb over my knuckles. Such a small, simple gesture, but it has the power to turn my knees to jelly. It's a good thing we're sitting down, or I might hit the floor.

"You know, there's something I wanted to discuss with you."

He grunts softly, pushing his plate away like he's ready for business. "Okay. Let's hear it."

"It's not that serious," I tell him, giggling at his sudden change. "Stand down."

"I'll be the judge of that," he retorts with a twinkle in his eye.

"I kinda sorta hinted to Mom that we made our relationship official."

Right away, he grins knowingly. "And when did she schedule the parade down Main Street? I imagine it would take time to get a brass band together."

"Wow. You are extremely full of yourself."

"Not full of myself," he replies, lifting a shoulder. "But I know she likes me. And let's face it, I'm a catch. The total package."

"I had no idea your ego was this big." I sit back, folding my arms, fighting off a grin.

"Let's look at the facts. I'm young and healthy. I'm a business owner. A respected member of the community. I don't have any bad habits."

"No comment," I murmur.

His eyes narrow. "Name one bad habit."

I hold up a finger. "You take too long in the bathroom."

"Compared to who?"

Two fingers. "You often have flour on your clothes." I reach out and run a hand over his short, chocolate-brown locks. "And crumbs in your hair."

"Call it an occupational hazard."

Three fingers. "And you are entirely too charming."

"If being a charmer is wrong, I don't wanna be right."

"And I wouldn't change it for anything," I assure him, getting serious again. "What I'm getting at is this, you have been invited to dinner at Mom's house."

I thought the invitation might please him. I didn't know it would make him smile from ear to ear the way he is now. "Really?"

"Really. Do you think you could handle that? You know she's the queen of invasive questions."

"That, I can handle."

I wish I could say the same for myself. I'm thirty years old and should be beyond getting embarrassed by my mom when there's a boy around, but then my mother should be past the point where she asks probing questions about issues that are none of her business. "I don't think you have any idea of what you're agreeing to."

"Life is the most fun that way," he counters with a gleam in his eye. "I mean, think about it. It's the challenge that makes life interesting. The unknown. I'll brace myself for personal questions. And I'll make sure to bring dessert, homemade. Just in case she wonders whether her little girl will be well fed once she offers your dowry and asks me to sign a marriage contract."

"You know what? Dinner's off."

"Nope. Too late," he teases, while all I can do is groan. The thing is, he only thinks he's joking. I would not put it past Mom to do exactly what he just described.

We both sigh softly when my phone rings. It's Captain Felch, and I wince apologetically. "Sorry, he never calls me unless it's important."

"I get it." He gathers our plates together and takes them behind the counter while I answer the call.

"Captain?"

"Sorry to bother you," he offers. Right away, I hear concern in his voice. "I'm going to need you here at the station."

"What's wrong?" I'm already grabbing my coat from where it hangs over the back of my chair.

"Looks like a young mother went missing on her run this morning."

5

ALEXIS

The Lawrence family lives in a huge, tasteful house close to the outskirts of the town's wealthiest area. I wouldn't call it a mansion but it is definitely spacious, sprawling, and the pair of Lexus SUVs parked in the sweeping, wide driveway tells me Mr. Lawrence is doing pretty well for himself.

A man I assume to be Connor Lawrence is pacing back-and-forth on the front porch while talking on his cell. There are cute little touches here and there; a wooden sign with the word Welcome painted across it hangs over the front door, while the railing spanning the porch edge is wound with what looks like real garland in preparation for Christmas. There's more of the same garland sitting in a pile – I wonder if the plan was to continue decorating today before fate intervened.

"I'll call you back." He tucks his phone into the back of his khakis before running both hands through his golden blonde hair in a gesture of total helplessness.

"Who are you?" he asks right away, before I've had a chance to open my mouth. "Are you with the police? I already spoke with the deputies."

"My name is Agent Alexis Forrest. I'm with the FBI."

"The FBI? Who contacted the FBI?" He's jittery, suspicious, dark eyes narrowing while he backs away. Not a great sign.

"I happen to be in town on another case. Captain Felch asked me to come out and speak to you, take down your statement, get a feel for your wife and her schedule, that sort of thing."

"I see." He thrusts out a hand. "I'm sorry. Connor Lawrence. I should have started out with that."

"No need to apologize." I shake his hand and notice how clammy it is against my own. "Why don't we go inside?"

"I don't understand this." He opens the door and ushers me inside, talking a mile a minute. "This is so unlike Alyssa. But I can't imagine anything happening to her. Not around here, you know? That's the sort of stuff you hear about on the news. And if Alyssa is one thing, it's responsible. She keeps her eyes open. She's smart. She doesn't take risks."

I don't have the heart to tell him intelligence has nothing to do with whether or not a person can avoid tragedy. Sure, there are steps to take in hopes of avoiding a terrible situation, but there is really no way to guarantee it.

The inside of the house looks like something out of Architectural Digest, or maybe Better Homes & Gardens. It's immaculate, so clean I am amazed two children live here. "And where are your children right now?"

"They're with the neighbors. To them, this is a fun little adventure." He barks out a laugh. "Kids are lucky like that."

"Can you explain to me what happened?" I pull out my phone and explain, "I would like to record your impressions, so I don't miss anything."

He shrugs it off. "I got a call from the kids' preschool saying they were never picked up at three o'clock. That's not Alyssa. She is punctual to a fault. A total Type A personality. Always on top of things."

"Is she a homemaker, or does she work outside the house?"

"She had a job in PR before the kids came along, and then she poured all of that energy into our family from then on." When he turns partly away from me, he runs a hand under both eyes like he doesn't want me to see him tearing up.

"You say she's Type A. I guess that means she's pretty disciplined when it comes to her schedule."

"Oh, completely. And that was another thing that hit me. Normally, she cleans up the kitchen after she drops the kids off. That's her routine. I came home and she hadn't done anything. That's not like her, either."

"Could she have maybe done something unexpected? Does she ever veer from the routine?"

"Not to the point where she can't pick up the kids. And she would never go anywhere without her phone – not to mention the fact that her car is parked outside." He is either in deep denial or he's doing all he can to make it seem that way out of guilt. Not that I want to doubt him, but this would hardly be the first time a pretty, young mother went missing from the so-called perfect home. And more often than not, the husband had something to do with it. Not always. But often.

There's a framed photo of her and the kids on the quartz countertop. She's the all-American girl. Her shining brown waves and bright smile were inherited by both kids, who were in the middle of laughing uproariously when the shot was taken.

"Did she have any friends around here who may have picked her up, gone out for coffee?"

"That still doesn't explain why her purse is still here. Believe me, Agent Forrest," he adds. "I've asked myself all these questions already, trying to make sense of it. But there isn't any making sense of it. I've called all of her friends whose numbers I have, asking around in case somebody needed her. She's the kind of friend who'll drop everything when one of her girls needs help. It's clear something went wrong while she was running. She's missing."

"I noticed you have a Ring doorbell outside."

"Of course. I only called the police once I confirmed she didn't come home." There's a tablet propped near the stove and he picks it up, bringing it over to me and opening the app to go through the footage. So far, I don't notice any red flags. If there were something to conceal, he wouldn't be so open with allowing me to check out the video.

As I watch, the entire family leaves the house. Alyssa is bright and energetic. Her dark brown ponytail swings back-and-forth as she leads those adorable kids to her SUV. Connor emerges from the house behind them and locks the door, then takes the same route to his car.

A half-hour later, Alyssa returns. She's humming to herself—I vaguely recognize the tune, something from the eighties, something Dad loves. She doesn't look worried or stressed at all. There's no looking over her shoulder, no sign of nerves. To her, it's just another day.

After another ten minutes, she emerges again, this time dressed in thick leggings, a hoodie, running shoes. She does a short stretching routine in view of the camera before inserting AirPods into her ears and starting off, jogging down the driveway.

Connor releases a groan. "Why did you have to go? If only she had stayed home."

"Is she a regular runner?"

"She ran every day before the kids were born, then was more sporadic about it for a long time. It's only been over the past few weeks that she's rededicated herself to it. Running clears her head and keeps her energy up."

"I've got to give her credit. I'm a runner myself, and I've fallen out of my own routine. All this snow doesn't help matters."

Finally, the camera picks up motion at a quarter-to-four, when Connor pulls up with the kids in his SUV. Alyssa never returned.

"Do you mind if I take a look around the house?" I ask once he sets down the tablet with a heavy sigh.

"No, of course. Whatever you need." He follows me, though, but I still don't get a bad impression from him. He's more like a worried child fretfully following somebody because they don't know what else to do. He's hoping for reassurance, for me to tell him everything will be fine. I wish I could.

"You have a very beautiful home," I tell him, even if I doubt the observation is any help at a time like this.

"You can give all the credit to my wife. She made this a *home*."

"You must've participated somehow, right? What is it you do for a living?"

"I'm a dermatologist."

I pause at the grand staircase and turn to him. "Oh, so it's Dr. Lawrence."

He shrugs. "I mean, yeah, but I didn't want to come off sounding pretentious."

"Which is exactly why I don't introduce myself as a doctor – Psychology," I add as his brows lift in a silent question. "And where were you today?"

"At the office. I spend more time there than I do here anymore." When I raise my brows the way he did, he sighs. "My partner and I are in the process of building our business. It's meant a lot of extremely long days. I had patients all morning, and my schedule was full through the end of my day before I got the call from the school."

"And what time is that, normally? The end of your day."

"Lately, it's been around nine o'clock. Our office closes at eight, but there are always stragglers at that time of night. That, plus things sometimes get backed up, appointments take longer than they should and it snowballs. But tonight, I was striving to be home by six."

"And why is that?"

"Can I ask what this has to do with Alyssa's disappearance?" The fact that he's waited this long to ask that question surprises me.

"I'm only trying to get a feeling for the nature of your relationship, what Alyssa's mental state may have been when she left for her run."

"No matter what was happening around here, she wouldn't run off. That's not Alyssa."

"I'm sure you're right. Still, it helps if I can get a full picture."

He grinds his teeth and jams his hands into his khaki pockets, lowering his gaze until he's staring at the shiny, hardwood floor. "It's taken a toll on us, honestly. Not that we were considering anything drastic, mind you. This is how it always goes for people in healthcare, especially when they're building a new practice. Impossibly long hours, distraction, that sort of thing. Today, I managed to stick around long enough to be home when Alyssa took the kids to school, but I'm usually out the door before they are. Last week, she showed me a calendar on which she had left a red X on the days when I got home too late to tuck the kids into bed. There were a lot of them."

"It's difficult when your schedule is crunched. Trust me, I can relate." Can I ever. How many times have I thanked my lucky stars that Mitch is as understanding as he is? I wonder what would happen if we added kids to the mix.

"She's been overwhelmed. She wants to start getting ready for the holidays, and of course she wants to turn the house into a showplace. I made the mistake of suggesting she not go all out and drive herself to the brink of insanity, and you'd think I suggested we skip the holiday entirely."

He looks around, his brow creased, his eyes pained. "I should've offered to help. That was what she wanted. That's all she ever wants. Some help. She accused me of not being around enough to help with the kids, and of course, I pointed out that I'm around on the weekends, but she said that's not enough. That the kids deserve more than a weekend dad."

"But you're working hard."

"You're right. I am. I'm trying to build something for all of us. It won't always be this way – I tried to tell her that, and I think we worked it out. She understands. Once the practice is on solid footing, I can sit back and reap the rewards. We all can."

Here comes the tough part. "I'm going to ask you something, and I hate to ask it, but it's pretty much standard."

He holds up a hand, shaking his head. "I wasn't having an affair. I have never been anything but faithful to my wife. There's not even so much as a flirtation going on with the receptionist. Ask anybody."

"And your wife?"

"Alyssa would never." He is adamant, shaking his head harder. "Her parents split up because of her father's infidelity. That was one of the defining situations of her life. I mean, we barely knew each other when she swore – completely unsolicited – that she would never do to her partner or her children what her father did."

All at once his eyes well up. "She's probably hurt somewhere. I should be out there looking for her! She might've broken something, slipped and fallen and hit her head, anything is possible."

"And I promise you, we already have cars out there, looking for her. If that's the case, and she was injured, they're going to find her."

Wringing his hands, he insists, "They have to. They just have to. I don't work without her, you know what I mean? None of us do. She is the heart of the family. She's our glue." He presses his lips together, his chin trembling, before he turns away and releases a shuddering sob.

6

ALEXIS

After my chat with Connor, I step outside and walk down to the end of the driveway. There are two squad cars parked down the street, and I watch as a deputy emerges from a house across from the Lawrences. When he sees me, he lifts a hand to grab my attention, then waves me over. I trot across the road, careful of the slick conditions thanks to a slick, wet snow that fell last night, before meeting him in the driveway.

"This one's a real character." He stands with his back to the house and jerks his head in the direction of a dark red front door hung with a cheerful wreath. "Mrs. Strasburg. Retired school teacher, her husband was a lawyer. He retired just two months before he had a massive heart attack. She doesn't like the woman who lives next to her, because she wears revealing outfits when she does her gardening, and she doesn't trust the family three doors down in the other direction, because their kid has tattoos. Would you like to know anything else about her or the neighborhood?"

"My gosh," I whisper, laughing softly. "Did you get her entire life story?"

"I'm pretty sure that was her goal. Anyway, she sees everything around here. She organized the neighborhood crime watch and everything, and likes sitting by the window to make sure there aren't any strange cars going up and down the street."

"In a situation like this, that could be helpful." Though on the other hand, I can imagine her neighbors becoming fed up with her. The word *busybody* comes to mind.

"She's all yours. I'm going to move onto the next house, see if they noticed anything." He smirks before starting off. "Maybe I'll get lucky and see one of those revealing outfits."

Meanwhile I brace myself, rolling my shoulders back before finishing the walk up the drive and knocking at the front door. It opens almost instantly, like she was waiting on the other side. She probably was. "My, aren't you pretty!"

Wow. That came out of nowhere. "Thank you," I reply with a gentle laugh. "Aren't you sweet? My name is Alexis, and I understand your name is Mrs. Strasburg."

Mrs. Strasburg has a head of thick, shining white hair that is absolutely striking, especially when paired with her pale blue eyes. Shrewd eyes – I doubt they miss a thing. She must've kept her husband on his toes. The fact that it only took two months of retirement for him to pass away ... One could make the argument that it was healthier for him to be at work all day.

"I already told that young man everything I know, but I'm happy to tell you the same thing." She steps back and waves me inside. The house is similar in build to the Lawrence home, but there are enough differences to tell me this was a different model. That's the way it is in many developments – you get a choice of three or four different versions of a house, rather than everybody looking exactly the same.

This house has a much more lived-in feeling to it compared to the Lawrences' perfectly curated, Instagram-worthy appearance. There are cozy touches like a colorful afghan draped across the back of a sofa, a sewing machine on the dining room table along with bolts of fabric, and what has to be hundreds of books lining an entire wall of the living room in which Mrs. Strasburg and I take a seat.

"I am envious of your library," I admit, nodding toward the wall. "That is a goal of mine, truly."

"You're very young. You have plenty of time to collect all these volumes. My husband and I shared a passion for reading."

"What did you do for a living?"

"I was a teacher at Hawthorne Academy."

"I'm familiar with it. I grew up in Broken Hill."

"Did you, now?"

"But I went to Broken Hill High," I explain. "Anyway, I understand you have some information about what happened today."

She clicks her tongue, shaking her head. "I wondered to myself whether it was a good idea for Alyssa to go on her run today. I was glad for her when she began running – she needs something for herself. Heaven knows she's the ideal mother and homemaker."

"So you're very familiar with her?"

"We've shared coffee a few times. She made it a point to invite me to little Hannah's fourth birthday party this past summer. The children are happy and healthy and both of them are bright as a button. They're always immaculately dressed and are terribly polite."

"I got the impression Mrs. Lawrence is very devoted to her family."

"That's putting it lightly. She adores those children."

"So, you said you saw her leaving for her run today?"

"Oh, yes. The roads are so slick, I wanted to call out to her and ask if she might want to skip a day. I figured I didn't want to be a busybody, so I kept my thoughts to myself." And I, in turn, bite my tongue rather than point out she's already earned the name. "Usually, she comes back around the time *Murder, She Wrote* starts. I watch it every weekday morning at ten."

"Oh, I like that show."

"I adore it. Mind you, some of the situations are a bit far-fetched, but it's comforting. I was already at the end of the episode before I realized I never saw Alyssa return."

"You might have missed her. She could've taken it a little slower or even shortened her route once she realized the condition of the roads."

"I checked my security footage to be sure. When Connor came home with the kids, I knew something had to be wrong. He would never go to pick them up during the day. He's much too busy with his work. That was what inspired me to take a look and see if Alyssa had returned, but she never did."

She clicks her tongue and frowns. "If something like this can happen to a sweet girl like her, it could happen to anyone. I hope it's only something like a slip and fall. That, she could make it through. She's young and healthy. But ..."

She heaves a sigh and shakes her silvery head. "You just can't be too careful nowadays, can you? There's danger all around."

Putting it mildly.

7

ALEXIS

Just when I thought I had my day planned out.

Originally, I intended to get on the phone with the parents of another one of Andrew Flynn's potential victims. Katie and Paul Roche lost their son Mark back in 2002. He was twelve years old and he'd gone out to ride his bike, the way kids do all the time.

He never came home. His bike was found half-submerged in a pond two days after his disappearance, and his body was found twenty miles away three days later.

My immediate inclination is to dismiss Mark as one of Andrew's victims – he doesn't fit the profile, He's not only younger than Andrew's usual victims, but he was also male. It isn't unlike a serial killer to switch things up sometimes, but I'm still wary of drawing parallels where there might not be any. His photo was in the cabin along with Maddie's and so many others, though, which is why I take the phone number from the information the Bureau uploaded to a secure, shared drive and dial it. I only hope his parents aren't too shocked at my sudden contact.

While the phone rings, my attention is split between little Mark and Alyssa Lawrence. Was Connor telling the truth back there at the house? It's very easy for a spouse to tell their side of the story and make it sound legitimate when their partner isn't around. There was no way for Alyssa to offer the other side of the story—and there always is one. Are they a happy couple? Or did Connor tell me what he knew I wanted to hear? If he planned this, he would've had plenty of time to practice the grieving spouse act.

"Hello?" A woman's voice rings out on answering my call.

"Hello. I'm calling to speak to either Katie or Paul Roche."

She hesitates for a moment before clearing her throat. "I'm Mrs. Roche. Who is this?"

After introducing myself, I get down to the reason for my call. "Mrs. Roche, I understand you lost your son, Mark, back in 2002."

"That's right," she answers, her voice stiff.

"I'm investigating a series of kidnappings and murders, and I was wondering if you and your husband could spare a little time to get together so we can discuss the details of your son's case."

"His case?" She blurts out a disbelieving laugh. "You might be the first person to ever call it a case."

"What do you mean, if you don't mind me asking?"

"At first, the cops wanted to believe he ran away." She's bitter, after all these years. I can't blame her. Nearly a quarter of a century has passed, but I doubt any parent would get over the sort of loss she's endured no matter how much time goes by. "No matter how many times we told them Mark would never run away for real, that he was a good kid and only went to his friend's house, they practically laughed us off and patted us on the head. They were so sure of themselves, so smug and snide. And what happened? My little boy turned up dead. Maybe if they had taken us seriously in the first place, they could've found him in time."

"I'm very sorry to hear that. I wish there were more I could say, but I know nothing can take that away. I have reason to believe the same individual was responsible for not only Mark's murder, but for a series of crimes before and after that time. I'm trying to find out everything I can about the people involved in hopes of discovering something they might have had in common. Do you think we could meet sometime soon? Would that be alright?"

"You mean, you might actually find out what happened to my son?" Her voice breaks a little at the end, and I give her a moment to gather herself before she continues. "Yes. Absolutely. You name the time, and we will be available."

"Thank you, ma'am." We make plans to meet tomorrow and she promises she and her husband will be home and waiting. I'm barely off the phone with her before my cell rings with a call from Mitch. It's that kind of day. Never a quiet minute.

"How's it going?" he asks. I told him before leaving the shop about the captain's call and why it was so important for me to leave in a hurry.

"Unclear," I report. "One step at a time. What's up? How are you?"

"I've got a little bit of egg on my face."

"Why? What do you mean?"

"Well, I'm not sure when your mother planned on getting together for dinner, but it just hit me that I have that conference in Bangor next week."

Of course. He told me about it, but I was too busy lamenting the idea of sitting down to dinner with both him and Mom to remember. "That's exactly when she was hoping to have you over." And it's funny how at a time like this, it even matters when he comes over. I have a disappearance on my hands, not to mention a dozen murders to investigate. Including my sister's. How lucky am I to worry about something this relatively trivial?

"I could do tonight," he offers.

Tonight? My stomach drops. "Oh, Mitch …"

"Or we can wait until I get back. I only wanted to give you the heads up, to give your mom some warning. You know me. I'm easy."

His sweetness loosens the pressure inside my skull. "I know you are. Okay. I'll give her a call and let her know. Maybe she can whip up a feast for us tonight." And maybe that's exactly what I need. I doubt I'll have the wherewithal to make pleasant conversation when I'm already running on fumes after crisscrossing town, but it could be nice to have an excuse to share a bottle of wine and eat some good food tonight. An excuse to unwind.

Or maybe that's what I need to tell myself as I place a quick call to my mother.

"Oh, that's short notice," she points out, as if I need to be told. "But I'm nothing if not flexible. You tell that little hunk of a boyfriend of yours he is more than welcome to come over tonight for dinner."

"Can you please not call him my little hunk of a boyfriend?" I whisper, careful to lower my voice so I'm not overheard.

"I'm only telling the truth."

"Just the same. It kind of creeps me out a little bit."

"Fine, fine. I'll pretend he's a dog. Would that make you feel better?"

"Yes, so much better." She is too much sometimes. All the time, really. "And he'll bring dessert. What time should I tell him?"

"Eight o'clock?" It's just past five now. I confirm for her, then shoot Mitch a text. He immediately replies with a thumbs up emoji, then a cake emoji. I hope that means we're having cake tonight. Now, all I have to do is actually get out of here in time, or else I just set my boyfriend up on a date with my mother.

Unfortunately, when a deputy approaches the room still being used as my makeshift office, it doesn't seem like my day is going to end anytime soon. "Agent Forrest, I have somebody out here. She said she has information about Alyssa Lawrence. A friend of hers."

"Thank you." I follow him out to the waiting area near the entrance, and though there are a handful of people sitting around, I get the feeling the blonde in the leggings and Ugg boots is the woman I'll be meeting with. Her long, glossy blonde waves shine almost as bright as the glare of fluorescent light reflecting off her big sunglasses. She sips something out of a Stanley Quencher cup and taps freshly manicured nails against her knee.

She screams money and privilege, in other words, but that's nothing new around here. What piques my interest most is the fact that she came in without being asked to do so.

"Excuse me," I offer on reaching her. "I'm Alexis Forrest. Are you here to discuss Alyssa Lawrence?"

She stands, nodding firmly. When she switches the cup from her right hand to her left, I'm nearly blinded by a stunning diamond ring. "Elizabeth Currid. I'm friends with Alyssa. I heard she's gone missing."

"That's right."

She perches her sunglasses on top of her head and her blue eyes narrow. "I want to make sure you know everything about what's going on in that house, and that marriage."

8

ALEXIS

"**M**rs. Currid. Right this way." It doesn't seem right, taking her to an interrogation room when she's not being interrogated. I don't want her feeling uncomfortable, either, which I can only imagine she would feel in such an environment. She's anxious enough already, almost like a coiled spring ready to pop. I want to believe it's all a result of her being worried about her friend, but she was practically hissing like a snake when she mentioned the Lawrences and their marriage.

"I hope this is alright for you," I offer once she's entered the meeting room. Normally, this is where higher level meetings take place – city government, officials, council members, that sort of thing. It's not usually put in use for the sake of keeping an anxious stay-at-home mom calm and willing to talk.

"Can I get you some coffee?" I ask, gesturing toward my own cup on the coffee table set up in front of a leather sofa.

"No, thanks." Elizabeth holds up her cup. "Already way ahead of you. I don't normally ingest caffeine this late in the day, but something tells me I won't be getting much sleep tonight, anyway. Might as well stay alert and productive rather than stare at the ceiling all night long, wondering what happened to Alyssa."

She places her Louis Vuitton bag on the table before settling in, crossing her legs and sipping from her straw. I sit a few feet away, my body angled toward hers. I place my phone between us and explain that I would like to record this for the sake of keeping everything straight. "Sure, whatever it takes. I want to make sure nothing I say gets misconstrued or misremembered, anyway."

She's frank, to the point, and clearly intelligent. I need to figure out the best way to approach this without spooking her or getting too far off-topic. It's the firm set of her jaw and the way her eyes are still narrowed in what could be anger or at least suspicion that makes me wary.

"Mrs. Currid. Outside, you told me you were friends with Alyssa. About how long have you known her?"

"Only since the beginning of the school year. Her Dylan is in the same class as my Benjamin, and we wound up getting closer when we both started serving on the PTA."

"Oh, I wasn't aware that Mrs. Lawrence was on the PTA at the school."

"Are you kidding? She's a force of nature." Admiration rings out in her voice, fresh and almost fierce. She has to defend her friend somehow. "It's a private school, you know? Parent involvement is important. Coming up with ideas for fundraisers, that sort of thing. She's a genius, I swear."

"From what I understand, she once had a career in public relations."

"Right, and she told me she really liked being able to put some of that skill into her life again."

Interesting. This is the first I've heard of Alyssa maybe not being quite as perfectly content as she's been described. Is she satisfied, living as a stay-at-home mom? "So the two of you got closer."

"Oh, yeah. In fact, we were all going to go out to Starbucks this morning, and I invited her, but …"

Her eyelids flutter, and along with them her fake lashes. She looks down at her lap, toying with her straw. "I wish I had made sure she came. But she said she had to get home for a run. I mean, once she gets an idea in her head, you don't get in her way. But I really, really wish I had tried harder."

"You couldn't have known."

"Anyway," she continues, " we usually get together for coffee or lunch two or three times a week. Sometimes there's a group of us, sometimes it's only the two of us. And when it's the two of us, we usually start talking about personal things. I got the feeling she needed somebody to confide in. She always said she didn't have a lot of close female friends anymore."

Interesting. Did Connor take that away from her? I didn't get that vibe from him – the controlling husband, the dominating partner who refuses to let his wife have a life outside the home. Then again, abusers are skilled at hiding their true nature from the rest of the world.

"And what sort of things did she tell you?"

"I'll tell you one thing, it wasn't going well with her and Connor." She gives me a look that's heavy with meaning.

So Alyssa's problems were deeper than a simple calendar with red Xs marking the days when she felt neglected by her husband. "About how long has it been since things took a turn? Do you know?"

"In the beginning, she would mention his long hours, how she never saw him, how he was always too busy to help out around the house. With the kids, you know. And she always understood why, but that didn't make it any easier to deal with." She sips her drink and I wait, letting her take her time. I don't want to push her. She may turn out to be a gold mine.

"But the past month or so," she continues, "she's been getting more agitated and frustrated. I guess there's only so much you can handle before you have to say enough."

"Of course."

"And then, there's been all the trouble with the IVF."

Stop the presses. "Pardon? They're pursuing IVF treatments?"

"Oh, yeah. They're trying for a third baby, but it hasn't been easy. As it is, Alyssa told me they were hoping to conceive naturally, starting about a year after Dylan was born, but month after month, no success. That was why they turned to IVF, but that hasn't been going well, either. And then, with the hormone treatments, she's felt all out of whack and everything. That was why she tried to get back into running, and that was why I didn't push any harder for her to come out with us today. Running helps her get her head together. Balances her out. It makes her feel like she's taking charge of her body when everything feels up in the air."

This is a much different version of Alyssa Lawrence than the one provided by her husband. So far, there's no reason to doubt both testimonies are true – Connor may be too distant, too emotionally unavailable for Alyssa to feel safe opening up to him about the way she's truly feeling, so she turns to her girlfriends. That wouldn't make her unique. There's a reason girl talk exists.

But he can't be completely oblivious to the changes her body is going through and the toll it's taken on her. Is he too busy being dazzled by her competency to notice she's a very real, live woman?

"I'm sure that can't make things any easier at home," I muse, hoping to encourage her to share more.

And it does. The woman's eyes practically light up. "She said it feels like he doesn't get it. Like he doesn't even try to understand. He's been so blasé about the whole process. She feels like she's going through all of this alone."

"Especially since he's out of the house so much of the time, I imagine."

"I mean, good for him, getting out there and taking a chance on his own practice. But come on. He's not curing cancer. He's injecting Botox and treating acne. Like, give me a break." She rolls her eyes dramatically and clicks her tongue in derision.

"Is that how Alyssa feels about it?"

"Listen. She's grateful for everything he gives her and the kids. For real. She doesn't take it for granted. But … she's frustrated. She's got two kids under five and that great, big house to take care of all by herself. Then whenever she mentions to Connor that things need to change, he just wants to throw money at the problem. Hire a housekeeper or a cook or a personal assistant. That's not what she wants. She just wants a husband who feels engaged. Like she's part of a team."

"I get the picture." And I feel for her.

"I mean, not to sound catty, but after our times together, I always feel so much more grateful for my husband. He works crazy long hours, but he's super engaged with the family. Like, I can't imagine having everything fall on me all the time."

"I've been to the house. I'm sure it's quite a challenge, but you would never know it takes any work."

"She's good at that." There is genuine fondness and maybe more than a little admiration in Elizabeth's voice and the way her eyes shine. Alyssa is someone she aspires to be.

"Let's get back to the IVF, if you don't mind. You said Alyssa was taking it hard, not having success with the treatments."

"Sure. She really wants this baby."

"Did she ever give you a sense of how Connor feels about it?" Considering he didn't mention it at all, I'm curious. Granted, there wasn't necessarily a reason for him to bring it up, but I think if I were trying to establish evidence of a warm and loving relationship with my spouse, I would be quick to point out that we were trying to have a third child together. A way of underlining the stability of the marriage.

Elizabeth snorts in derision and waves a hand. I wonder how she manages to lift it with a rock like that weighing it down. "Please. He couldn't care less."

"What makes you say that?" I ask. It's pretty clear from her attitude that she doesn't care for Dr. Lawrence, meaning I have to take her statements with a grain of salt. I would have anyway, but it seems even more important to keep a neutral stance before jumping to conclusions.

"He just doesn't seem into it. He straight-up told her they didn't need to keep trying. He's happy with the way things are, they don't need another baby. So that's been an issue, too. She's been trying to get him to care, to at least meet her halfway. It's been so hard for her to feel like she's alone."

We keep coming back to that word. Alone. This conversation is reshaping the image Connor and Mrs. Strasburg created. Now, I imagine a pretty young mother alone for most of the day in a big house. Even when she isn't alone, she feels that way, overwhelmed by her responsibilities, carrying everything on her own.

"All I'm saying is, don't let him fool you," Elizabeth warns. "He's a nice guy and everything, but it's like he has no empathy. Do you know what I mean? He can't see beyond what's important to him. That's something else they've been fighting about. Her trying to make him understand how she feels."

"Because his practice is what matters the most right now."

"Exactly. He can't see anything else but that. He thinks making money is, like, the only thing a wife wants from her husband. I mean, come on." She laughs, shaking her head. "Men can be so clueless."

"They can be, sometimes."

"Just, you know. You have to find her." The brash, confident demeanor melts away, and now she's a concerned friend. "She has so many people who love her."

I assure her we're doing everything we can before we leave the room and she heads out. And it's not a lie. We're doing everything in our power.

After speaking with Elizabeth, it's starting to look like doing everything in our power includes bringing Connor Lawrence in for questioning. Thanks to the picture Elizabeth painted, I now have to wonder if he didn't have a motive for getting his wife out of the picture. A wife who nags about his long hours, who doesn't understand how hard he works, who insists on having a third child at the sacrifice of their relationship.

It could be that he got tired of listening to it. He wouldn't be the first husband who did, and who then took things much too far.

9

ALEXIS

"How do you want to tackle this?"

I appreciate that Captain Felch gives me space to handle things my way. It's a professional courtesy, I'm sure. I'm the one with the Bureau training, I'm the one with a PhD that helps me relate to victims and perpetrators alike. From the beginning, he has been more than glad to step back and work with me instead of working against me like other established veterans might do. Plenty of cops resent the presence of outsiders poking around their town, but then I'm not really an outsider, am I? And if anything, there are things about this town I understand much better than he could, having grown up here. Knowing from experience how the town's idyllic nature can hide the darkness that sometimes lurks beneath the surface.

I pace his office, chewing my lip, going over everything I've heard so far today. "I won't get anywhere by pushing too hard. I want him to feel comfortable. We are on his side, after all. And he did strike me as being genuinely distraught today – I can play that up, offer sympathy, almost coddle him a little. Let him loosen up, remind him we're on his side."

"What does your gut say?"

That's not such an easy question to answer right away. "I got a sincere feeling from him earlier today, really," I muse. My conflicting impressions are beginning to reflect in a sense of something close to agitation. Like the feeling of wearing something that's a little too tight, or an itchy wool sweater. I'm all out of sorts, not quite comfortable.

"What you've heard since that has colored your opinion."

"It's opened a new avenue of possibility," I offer. "Does that make sense?"

"That makes perfect sense. And that's why I called you in when we got the report that she was missing."

"What do you mean?"

"You don't jump to conclusions."

"Isn't that sort of the point?" I ask with a soft laugh.

"Of course it is. Tell that to a jaded, twenty-five-year vet who has seen it all twice and can't be convinced there's any such thing as a nuance in a case like this. Right away, they might jump to the conclusion that Connor got rid of his wife because she nagged too much or put too much pressure on him. At least you're willing to explore before pursuing a theory."

"I appreciate that."

"I appreciate it, too," he chuckles. "And I trust you. Maybe I've come to rely on you a little too much."

I'm pleasantly overwhelmed and don't know what to say. That makes this the perfect time for Connor Lawrence to enter the interrogation room after being led past the window in the captain's office.

At first glance, he's still a confused, worried husband. There are circles around his eyes like he's been crying, which I would expect from a devoted husband at a time like this. "How do you fake that kind of worry?" the captain murmurs, practically echoing my thoughts before I have the chance to speak them out loud.

"You either have to be sincere, or a truly gifted sociopath."

"Let's find out which one he is."

I leave his office and cross the hall, and I note the curious look Andy Cobb wears when he notices me.

I sincerely hope he doesn't feel like starting his petty drama with me right now. It seemed we'd finally reached a point where he's let go of the need to mock me, but who's to say? Watching me work alongside the captain might rub him the wrong way. He might've imagined they were rid of me.

I don't have time for that now. Instead of asking Andy what he's looking at, I open the door to the interrogation room and step inside. Connor immediately registers recognition, and my appearance seems to loosen him up a little – his shoulders are no longer around his ears. He's dressed in the same clothes he wore earlier, a button-down and khakis. Now, there's a red stain on his shirt cuff that draws my attention straight away.

He notices where my gaze has landed and snickers. "This is what happens when I make dinner. At least I let Hannah bully me into wearing Alyssa's apron, or else I would be covered in splattered spaghetti sauce."

"Your daughter is four, if I understand correctly?" I laugh knowingly when Connor nods. "The intersection of improved verbal skills and a firm belief that things need to be done a certain way," I offer with a grin. "If that's how Mom always does it, that's how it has to be done."

"Exactly. But like I said, it saved my shirt." He looks down at his cuff, picking at the stain. "Not that it matters much."

"I'm sorry we had to bring you in. I know it can't be easy, with the kids and everything. You can't just pick up and go at a moment's notice."

"Mrs. Strasburg across the street was nice enough to offer to sit at the house for me. The neighbors have all been very helpful the past several hours."

I glanced up at one of the cameras mounted in the corner of the room, over Connor's head. I know Captain Felch is watching. "I had a few more questions I wanted to ask now that I've spoken to a couple of people who know Alyssa. Mrs. Strasburg has nothing but glowing things to say about her, which something tells me is a minor miracle, all things considered."

He snorts, gently rolling his eyes. "She's a nice woman. A good neighbor. But yeah, she also has a lot of opinions that she feels very strongly about."

"And you are very diplomatic," I offer before we share a soft laugh. "She praised the kids up and down, too. Obviously, you two are doing a great job with them."

"I really do wish I could take more credit, but I'm not exaggerating when I say it's all thanks to Alyssa. I don't know how she does it, honestly."

He sits back in the chair, heaving a sigh. "Please, tell me you've heard something. Anything."

"We're working on it. None of the officers on patrol found anything unusual when they canvassed your area. No signs of an accident, certainly no wounded runner waiting to be helped."

"And what does that mean?" His dark eyes move over my face, searching for answers. "Do you think she was ... taken? I mean, I don't even like to say it out loud, but do you think it's possible?"

"Unfortunately, anything is possible. Now that we've established it's unlikely Alyssa was injured somewhere along her route, it is looking increasingly likely that she met with foul play. I'm very sorry to have to put it that way."

He clasps his hands on the table. "How is that even possible?" he whispers, staring at his hands, trembling. "I mean, this is the twenty-first century. Nobody disappears without a trace. Can't you, I don't know, track her phone? She took it with her."

"We're looking into that, but if the phone has been powered down, there's no way of tracking its location."

"I can tell you, she wouldn't do that unless somebody forced her to. She's never out of touch. She wouldn't want to miss anything about the kids."

That could be the opening I need. "Speaking of your family … I understand the two of you have been trying for number three. That you've been going through IVF treatments."

His eyelids flutter, and his mouth works silently before he composes himself. "I guess you've been talking to her friends."

"I've had a conversation or two."

"Then I guess you know it's been unsuccessful so far." He shrugs. "I mean, it's not like a big secret. Plenty of couples go that route when they have trouble conceiving naturally."

"How has it affected your marriage?"

His shoulders have started creeping up again. "I don't know what you're talking about."

"Let's be realistic," I murmur, folding my hands on the table the way he has. "No, I've never gone through IVF treatments myself, but I know they can take a toll – mentally, physically, emotionally. It's a difficult process, especially when it's unsuccessful."

"Sure." He has truly shut down. I didn't think it would happen this soon.

I need to coax him back out of his shell. "I'm only trying to get a sense of what Alyssa may be going through right now."

"I'm telling you, she's not going through anything."

"I see. So she was glad the IVF hasn't worked so far?"

"Why are you harping on this?" He throws his hands in the air, snorting. "You should be out looking for her instead of harassing me about our personal life."

"It's not my intention to harass you." My voice is low, calm, and I make it a point to look him in the eye when I speak. "But as I said, this is all part of understanding Alyssa."

"Fine. Do you want to understand Alyssa?" Folding his arms, he sighs. "We just went through our second cycle. Two days ago, we got word that the latest embryo didn't implant." He swallows hard, but that's the extent of emotion he reveals.

"How did Alyssa feel about that?"

"How do you think? I mean, she's a strong woman," he insists. "She doesn't break down and weep. She doesn't let herself wallow – that's a word she uses a lot, wallowing. She refuses to do it. She always wants to push forward. But she was a little sad. Disappointed."

"And how did you feel about it?"

For the briefest moment, something like resentment hardens his features. He hates that I'm asking these questions. "Honestly?"

"Preferably."

"It's not that I was happy about it. I need you to understand that. I would've been thrilled if we had success. I was a little sad, too, but then I tried to take a more positive stance."

"How so?"

"I reminded my wife that we have two perfectly beautiful, healthy, brilliant kids. Kids who adore her, kids she adores. I would rather enjoy them than spend all this energy and money on trying to make a third."

It's a reasonable stance. "And how did she take that?"

He releases a silent laugh before shrugging. "Let's put it this way, we were going to go for a third cycle."

"I see."

"The way I was raised, we lived by an adage, happy wife, happy life."

"I've heard it."

"And that's all I want for her. I want her to be happy. I just wish she didn't feel like she needs something extra if she's going to be happy. I wish … she could be as happy as I am with the way things are now. But there are things I guess men will never quite understand." He says it with no hint of sarcasm, no bitterness. He's sad, if anything.

And I am no closer than before to getting a solid read on him.

10

ALEXIS

"That's it." I lean against the closed door to the captain's office and rub my temples, not that it does much to relieve the tension in my head. "So much for questioning him when he's about as helpful as a brick wall."

Captain Felch grunts out his own frustration. "He's either innocent, or he's been practicing this long enough to come off genuine."

"Do you believe him?" I ask.

"He's still a suspect," he allows as he sinks into his desk chair and taps his fingers on the reports spread out in front of him. "That's more a matter of proximity to the victim than the result of any evidence."

"The only thing I can find him guilty of as of this moment is being kind of a poor husband," I declare with a sigh. "And even then, I didn't pick up on any maliciousness or attempts at controlling her. He's just sort of clueless as of right now. If we find something else, that could change."

He eyes me shrewdly. "What does your gut say?"

I get where he's going with the question, but the only thing my gut is interested in right now is the fact that it's empty and the clock on the wall reads seven-thirty. I'm supposed to be at Mom's by eight.

"I don't get a gut feeling that he's behind this," I admit with reluctance. "Like you said, he could have been planning this for ages and gotten the whole act down perfect. We don't know yet. If it was him, it would more than likely mean hiring a third party to take care of it for him since he was in his office all day. I'm sure there are plenty of people who could provide a solid alibi."

"And the perp could be someone entirely unrelated to the Lawrences," he reminds me. "We can't afford to put all of our eggs in one basket."

"Thank you for reminding me." I straighten up and stretch before groaning. "I hate to run off, but I have plans that can't be changed."

"By all means. A date with Mitch Dutton?" When I raise an eyebrow, he shrugs good-naturedly. "Sorry. All the time you've been here, I've wondered if you had anything close to a personal life to offset all the misery we encounter. I am glad you do."

"Don't get ahead of yourself," I warn with a grimace. "I'm having dinner with Mitch ... and my mother."

"Dinner with Mom." He can barely hide a grin as he waves toward the door. "Don't let me keep you. Good luck to Mitch."

"And me?" I prompt.

"You, I'm not worried about it." He shoos me away again. "Hurry up. There's nothing worse than being left alone with your girl's parents while you're waiting for her to show up."

I wish I had a little more time to prepare myself for this, and that we could maybe have done this on a day when I haven't been running around like a chicken with my head cut off. Then again, when was the last time I didn't run around like that? There's no way of guaranteeing how things are going to go from day to day. The word *unpredictable* has been much too applicable lately.

I guess we may as well get it over with. The less time Mom has to prepare awkward questions, the better for all of us. Today's relatively balmy temperatures meant a lot of melting of snow and ice piled up along the sides of the roads, and now that the temperature has dropped, things are a little slick. I slide twice on my way to the car, the sort of close call that makes my heart thump while muscles I forgot I possessed tense up all at once.

Not that it's much of a difference from the rest of my body, since I'm already tensed up from head to toe. The extra time it takes for the car's heater to warm up allows me the chance to catch my breath, resting my head against the seat and closing my eyes before I begin to breathe slowly, deeply.

It's moments like this when I have to wonder what Mitch wants to do with me in the first place. Anybody can decide to leave work at work, to not bring it home with them, but I've never been that person. If we have any hope of a long-term relationship, I need to learn to compartmentalize better. Not that Mitch would ever ask me to stop talking about work. He knows how much it means to me. But that doesn't mean it has to rule our relationship.

The fact that I'm thinking that far into the future should startle and maybe even alarm me a little. but how could it when the idea feels so natural? Almost like, obviously, we're going to be together. Obviously, this is how it was supposed to be. Obviously, we were meant to reconnect during my return to town.

It's that thought, plus the notion of how awkward things could get if I show up late, that gets me moving. I pull out of the slick lot, glad to see one of the janitorial staff hauling out a bag of salt to treat the steps and sidewalk before I turn onto Main Street, which I'm glad to see was treated earlier in the day.

What kind of questions could Mom ask? I feel like I owe Mitch the favor of at least coming up with a few deflections, things that will distract her before she can truly humiliate either of us. Heck, maybe I'll announce a missing woman instead of talking about Mitch's goals or his intentions for us, or whether there's any history of terrible health problems in his family so she can know what to expect for her grandchildren someday down the line.

Once I turn away from Main Street and the woods to either side of the road grow thicker, I ease on the gas and flip on my high beams. This is exactly the sort of scenario car accidents are born from. There are no lights out here beyond those on the front of my Corolla, and those lights only serve to reveal the ice that's beginning to glisten on the pavement. The road bends and I move with it, biting my lip and praying there aren't any deer up ahead. I only release my held breath when I find the road clear of obstructions.

It's already a few minutes to eight, and I drum my fingers against the wheel, hoping she doesn't get weird tonight. That's what is at the heart of everything. I can take prying questions, I can take her not being able to pick up a hint. I can't take her drowning in the past, allowing her addiction to get a hold on her again. That, I would rather Mitch not be present for. If she felt stressed out over throwing dinner together at the last minute, would that maybe have been enough to throw her over the edge?

I feel the car beginning to drift before I consciously realize I hit a patch of ice. All at once, everything Dad ever told me about driving on ice comes roaring back — he wasn't around when I learned to drive, but he used to describe the process so one day I would know what to do.

Rather than try to steer in the opposite of the direction the car has drifted, I follow the car's motion, easing the wheel rather than cutting it, tapping the brakes rather than slamming on the pedal.

I still end up coming to a stop only feet from a mailbox, my heart in my throat, my hands wrapped around the wheel tight enough to make my joints ache. Yet I'm surprisingly clear headed. All of the anxiety has been wiped away.

Funny how it takes something like a close call to open my eyes to what matters. I'm getting myself upset over nothing. Mitch can handle Mom's insatiable curiosity, and she can handle hosting dinner. Someday, I'm going to have to stop worrying so much about everybody around me.

The rest of the drive goes by uneventfully, and I'm not surprised to find Mitch's car already parked at the curb. Mom likes to leave the car at the bottom of the driveway on nights like this, so there's no icy mess to worry about glazing it over in the morning. That gives me no choice but to pull in behind Mitch and take one last deep breath before opening the car door and forcing myself out into the cold night.

Here goes nothing.

11

ALEXIS

"That is fascinating." Mom is absolutely charmed by pretty much everything Mitch has to say, but she seems especially fascinated by the ins and outs of his business. "So you can send inventory back to the publisher if it doesn't sell? I always imagined bookstores kept all those unsold books... somewhere."

"You would be surprised how much doesn't get sold," he explains. No matter how many questions she asks, no matter how frankly silly some of them are, he treats her curiosity with kindness and patience. "And there are always new books coming out. We have to make room for those. But if we return the unsold books, we're refunded the money we spent on them."

"Oh, that's good to know. I can't imagine how you would make any money otherwise."

"It's a pretty great business." Mitch glances my way with a twinkle in his eye. He's loving this. Any opportunity to talk about his work.

"But it really has taken off since he built the café and started baking," I point out, since I like being able to brag about him.

"I can't wait to dig into that bundt cake you brought," Mom assures him before dishing herself another chicken cutlet and adding a little extra pasta alongside it. "Tell me. Have you ever considered having authors come in for signings and readings? I bet people in town would love it."

"I would love it, too," he confesses. "But we're sort of small time, all things considered. But I'm working on developing a few relationships."

She dabs the corners of her mouth with her napkin before pushing her chair back. "I'm going to refill my iced tea. Can I get either of you anything?"

After assuring her we're both fine, we smile at each other. "Hi," I whisper. It's the first moment we've had alone since I entered the house to find Mitch helping Mom set the table.

He grins before winking. Always the charmer. "Hi. How am I doing so far?"

"Are you kidding? You're amazing, but I'm not surprised."

Mom clears her throat loudly before re-entering the room, and I have to cover my mouth with my napkin to hide my laughter. What is this, a drawing room comedy being played to a full house? What did she think we could possibly get up to in the twenty seconds she was in the kitchen?

"I guess you must have nothing but interesting books to read in your downtime." Mom settles back in, ready for more information about him. It's like she's building a profile. "What's your favorite genre?"

Here I am, expecting him to say something like philosophy, non-fiction. He surprises me with his immediate answer. "Fantasy."

"Why didn't I know that?" I ask, propping my chin on my hand and forgetting about food for a second.

"You never asked." He winks at me before turning back to Mom. "I do most of my reading at the store, in our downtime. Like you said. I wasn't much of a fantasy reader before I took over the store, come to think of it. I had a customer come in about a year ago asking for a particular series that was popular at the time, and since he had been a good customer, I promised to order it for him. I ended up ordering a few extra copies and got totally sucked into the story, and I've never looked back. I enjoy diving into a new world."

"Now that I think about it, you do have a pretty big fantasy section." I use what's left of my bread to sop up the lemon sauce while making a mental note to find out which authors and series he likes best. I'd like to have some common ground between us, and I've never shied away from a thick book.

"I like to stock genre books. Romance, thrillers, mysteries. You would be surprised at the taste of some of Broken Hill's residents." He leaves it there, wiggling his eyebrows a little.

"Who would've thought owning a bookstore could be so full of intrigue?" I tease. I can't believe I'm actually sitting here feeling so lighthearted and relaxed. It would be one thing if we were imbibing, but I wouldn't dream of bringing alcohol into the house and possibly making things challenging for Mom.

Big surprise; there wasn't nearly as much for me to be worried about as I imagined there would be. I can relax and enjoy myself while drinking nothing stronger than iced tea.

"I can't tell you how nice this is." My mother wears a fond look as her gaze bounces between me and Mitch. "I can't help but feel a little sentimental. I look at the two of you now, but I see the kids you used to be. How is it you both got so much older, but I haven't aged a day?"

Mitch points to her with his fork. "You know, I was just saying to myself when I came into the house that you look younger than you did when I was in high school."

Even Mom has to laugh at that one, though she does shoot Mitch a sly grin. "Flattery will get you nowhere – at least, I think I heard that once. I've never found it to be true, personally. But I mean it," she insists as we laugh. "It's eerie in a way. You're both so grown up now."

She doesn't have to finish her thought. I can feel it without her needing to say a word. We grew up, but Maddie didn't. What would Maddie's life have been like if she had been given the chance to live it?

"I've been thinking a lot about Maddie lately," she admits with a faint smile. "I'm sorry. I don't mean to bring the room down."

"You didn't," Mitch tells her. "It's only natural."

"It's the sort of thing you never get over," she murmurs, staring at the platter in the center of the table. "You only learn to live with it. You can even get used to carrying the burden around with you. Then somebody says something or does something and it reminds you. Girl goes missing. That's sort of thing."

This is what I was worried about. I have nothing to hide from Mitch, goodness knows. We are well beyond that point. I was hoping she wouldn't feel so sad, though.

"And it's not fair to you," Mom continues, looking at me. "I don't want you to feel like you have to live for the both of you. But I would be lying if I said I don't think of your sister at times like this. You and Mitch have found something wonderful together – and don't get upset with me for saying it," she's quick to add, scowling at me from across the table. "If you can't see what a catch you have here, I've failed you as a mother."

"There is going to be no handling him after this, I hope you know that," I murmur, and he snorts softly.

Mom only offers a weak smile. "The point remains."

"Actually," I tell her, glancing at Mitch, "I've been meaning to mention that I reached out to another family. Parents of a girl who was lost years before Maddie. I feel like I need to do this."

"Do you mean all those pictures and articles you found at the cabin?" She folds her arms and rubs them briskly like she feels a sudden chill. Not that I would be surprised in this drafty old house, but I get the feeling it's more to do with the topic.

"Yes. I went back to the first case documented there. The family recognized the cabin and claimed they vacationed there, or at least very nearby. I might be getting closer to finding a connection. They could've known this man. And the next family I visit might also have known him. There could still be hope of finding the real killer."

I don't know what I expected. Certainly not applause or anything like that. I'm not deluded. I offered the information in the spirit of giving her a little hope, yet her frown deepens until it turns into something that looks more like fear. "What's the matter?" I ask, "I didn't mean to make you upset."

"I'm not upset," she's quick to insist. "But I am worried."

"About what?"

"About you, silly. What do you think? If this man is still out there somewhere, what happens if he finds out you're onto him?"

"I highly doubt that's going to happen." Yet when I look to Mitch for a little assistance, it's quickly clear I'm not going to get any from him on this particular topic. He looks just as concerned as she is, so he doesn't say a word. He settles for picking at what's left of his salad, carefully avoiding my gaze.

"Just the same," she insists. "I need you to promise me, Alexis. Do not take any unnecessary risks. Your sister is gone and heaven knows I'll spend the rest of my life missing her. So will your dad. So will you. And you can't bring her back. I won't have you risking yourself. Do I make myself clear?"

I did not have getting told off by my mother on my bingo card. I have to give it to her – she manages to surprise me. "I promise. No unnecessary risks. Just a few interviews, a little fact-finding. That's all I'm doing."

"Why do I get the feeling you're telling me what you think I want to hear so I'll get off your case?" Mom looks at Mitch, jerking her head in my direction. "Does she do this to you?"

"Yes, Mitch," I turn to him, folding my arms and arching an eyebrow. "Do I do this to you?"

He looks at Mom. He looks at me. He clears his throat. "Can I plead the fifth?"

12

KILLER

W hat a cozy scene it must be up in that big, rambling place. The three of them seated around the table, enjoying a homemade meal. Like something out of a Hallmark movie or an old Norman Rockwell illustration.

And here I sit, watching from afar the way I've watched so many families for so long. I've had new interests over the years, I've drifted from place to place either out of boredom or necessity. I've had my head turned by interesting faces, intriguing smiles. That's all it takes sometimes. A stranger looking at me a certain way on a certain day. That's all it can take for my interest to grow until I don't have a choice but to absorb every part of that person. Until I can practically exist in their life.

Over the years, though, on quiet nights spent lying in bed, my thoughts have always drifted back to

Madeline. I never did care for the name Maddie – it didn't suit her. She was a girl of rare wisdom. Intelligence. Maturity. Years later, she's still the only one who never panicked beyond the understandable surprise when we first came face-to-face and I brought her home with me. There was no pleading, no weeping or wasted energy. There was no reason to be rid of her quickly. That's another reason she stands out in my memory, the amount of time we spent together. I was sorry to end our acquaintance.

It's almost like I have her back, only in the form of her younger sister.

She thinks she's on to me. The thought makes me laugh to myself as I stare up at the house. As if this girl could hope to pin me down when an entire generation of cops and Feds haven't been able to do it. It's personal for her. I can even respect that, truly. She has a strong sense of right and wrong. A solid moral compass. I might not be able to relate, but I can respect it.

It's easy to respect her rather than take her as a serious threat when I know she doesn't have the first clue how close she's been to me so many times. We've been together many more times than that single meeting at the Academy. I haven't been able to help it, though I know I should. I'm walking a thin line and might be tempting fate. There's a reason I've flown under the radar all this time. I've been careful, I've kept to myself, I've rarely taken chances. And when necessary, I've changed my appearance. At this very moment, I wear a beard and my hair brushes my shoulders. Not my favorite look, but it's different enough from my appearance while I was employed at the Academy that I've moved unnoticed around the periphery of Alexis Forrest's life without her noticing. I've stood behind her in line at the pharmacy. I've followed her to and from her boyfriend's, her mother's, the police station. She's tempted me that deeply.

She thinks she can catch me when she can't recognize me? It's laughable. Almost enough to make me want to pat her on the head, the way I did when Madeline told me stories about her during those long, intimate hours we spent together at the cabin. Those memories are part of the reason why I've never been able to fully distance myself from the area. I'd like to revisit those days, to live through the memories the way I would flip through a favorite book. *My sister is probably a genius. She's always reading. She can always tell when people are lying. She is so funny, and she looks up to me, but sometimes I wish I was more like her.*

Someday soon, I'm going to tell Alexis all the things her sister told me about her. I'll save it for the end, for those final moments before it comes time for the inevitable. And that time always comes.

I wonder which of those upstairs bedrooms once belonged to Madeline. She described it to me in great detail, as she did the rest of the house. She even told me about the stained glass rose in the attic. I admire it now as I have so many times. It's a way of feeling connected to my favorite friend – and her little sister, who has become more important than ever before. Sometimes I imagine Alexis up there. Late at night, when I'm alone, I close my eyes and picture her in that bedroom with its pink curtains. I imagine her as the little girl she was back then, ten years old, full of hope for the future, so sure her wonderful family would support her always and never be broken.

"You want so much to meet me again," I murmur, imagining Alexis here with me now. I feel so close to her, knowing she must have been nervous to have dinner with her mother and her boyfriend. What a special occasion. " But not quite yet, little Alexis. Not until I have a little more fun."

That's something she'll never understand, no matter how many degrees she earns. The thrill of being part of her world without her knowing it. Testing myself. Seeing how close I can come. Brushing against her in passing, getting away with it again and again.

I might become addicted to the thrill. I might already have.

The way I've become addicted to her.

Settling back with a smile, I entertain myself with thoughts of how she'd react if she knew the man who blew her life apart is sitting at her front curb.

13

ALEXIS

"Oh, Dr. Lawrence won't be in today." The wide-eyed young woman at the reception desk shakes her head before biting her lip like she's concerned. She might be wondering why she allowed me inside the office in the first place when they don't open for another twenty minutes. "With his wife missing and everything, he's in no condition to come in and work."

Wow. I'm not sure how to answer that. "I'm aware," I eventually decide to explain rather than ask why in the world she thinks I've stopped by. "And that's why I'm here, hoping to speak to you and Dr. Lawrence's partner, and anyone else who might be able to give me insight."

Her thick lashes flutter. "Insight into what?"

"Anything, really. I would like to know as much as I can about Dr. Lawrence – and his wife, if any of you are familiar with her."

The girl's name tag reads *Meredith*. She's very pretty, in her late twenties, and polished to the hilt. There is not so much as a single line or wrinkle in her smooth complexion. Is she already getting treatments here at the office? She couldn't possibly need them at her age, but then I guess there's a certain image that has to be projected.

She flips her perfectly blown out ash blonde hair over one shoulder. "Dr. Chetty told me to let him know when you're here. He wants to come out and talk to you."

"Terrific." I worried he might be resistant. "Do you have any other staff here at the office?"

"There's Bridget. She's part-time, but she's here today. I think she's in the break room."

Meredith gets up to gather everyone together so we can talk before the office opens to patients. The phone rings while she's away from her desk, but I hear her somewhere in the office, probably having picked up an extension. She is warm, but straightforward, letting whoever is on the other end of the call know Connor won't be in today and that there's no confirmation of when he'll return to the office.

As I wait, I look around at the framed magazine covers and certificates hanging on the walls of the waiting room. Most of them feature Dr. Chetty, an attractive, older man with salt-and-pepper hair and a warm smile. He's been named the area's top dermatologist three times, according to the certificates, and has been featured in magazines related to his field.

"Agent Forrest? Stuart Chetty."

I turn and am instantly curious about the man coming toward me with one hand outstretched. He is the man from the magazine covers, no doubt about that, but he doesn't look the way I would expect a popular, respected dermatologist would. There's nothing flashy about him, nothing false. The lines on his forehead and at the corners of his eyes make sense when paired with his graying hair and the bifocals he wears. It looks like the magazines Photoshopped his face, since there wasn't a wrinkle to be found.

"It's a pleasure to meet you, but I'm sorry it has to be under these circumstances." That's as much as I manage to get out before Meredith returns, this time coupled with a freckled girl who looks young enough to be in college.

"Have you heard anything about Alyssa?" Dr. Chetty asks in a voice heavy with concern.

All three of them sigh when I shake my head. "Unfortunately, we haven't. There have been teams sweeping the area since yesterday afternoon, and no one has picked up a sign of her anywhere so far."

"When I think about those poor kids ..." He shakes his head and clicks his tongue mournfully.

"And how is Dr. Lawrence?" Meredith asks, chewing on her bottom lip.

"He's understandably distressed." It seems the safest thing to say, and I'm sure it's true. He must be distressed, whether or not he was responsible for Alyssa's disappearance. He's either wondering where she is or wondering if he's going to get away with it.

"How long have you worked with Dr. Lawrence?" I ask Meredith.

"I was hired when Dr. Lawrence and Dr. Chetty opened their practice," she explains. "And that was ..."

"A little less than a year ago," Dr. Chetty confirms. "Time flies, doesn't it?"

"And you, Bridget?" I ask, turning to the girl who keeps shifting her weight from one foot to the other. I doubt that means she has the first clue about Alyssa. I'm an FBI agent, and the badge tends to freak people out sometimes.

"I only started working part-time this semester," she explains in a voice tight with nerves.

"I see. And how would you describe Dr. Lawrence? It's all right," I insist, looking at all three of them in turn. "Everything you say here stays anonymous."

Bridget shrugs first. "He seems … nice. Everybody likes him. Whenever I cover the front desk for Meredith, the women who call request him all the time."

Dr. Chetty flinches slightly but says nothing. I wonder what that means. Is he wondering why he's not as popular? Or does he know the girl just tripped over her tongue? I'm sure she meant nothing by it, but she's managed to make Connor look like a ladies man.

"He has a way of making you feel at ease," Meredith explains. "He's really good with the patients. They trust him – and Dr. Chetty," she quickly adds with a faint smile toward her other boss. "It's a really great working environment. Probably the best I've ever been part of." Either she's sincere and feels like she needs to defend Connor somehow, or she's praising her boss while in his presence. Either way, I'm not sure I can take what she says at face value. She's going a little over the top.

"I understand you tend to work long hours around here," I continue, turning toward the doctor. "It must be exhausting."

"It can be, but there is a bigger purpose at stake. And I made sure Connor understood what we were getting into when we decided to pair up in this partnership."

"Was Dr. Lawrence in the office yesterday?" I know the answer, but I want it confirmed. And I would like to hear from them say the time of his departure.

"He was booked solid," Meredith reports. "I had to call, like, eight people to reschedule. It was a nightmare." She must realize her awkward mistake – after all, it's a little more of a nightmare to come home and find your wife missing. Her face flushes to the roots of her hair before she averts her gaze.

"Around what time did he leave the office?" I ask, looking around.

It's Dr. Chetty, who responds, stroking his chin and narrowing his eyes. "It was around three-fifteen, I think. I remember that, because Alyssa was supposed to pick the kids up at three, and it seemed so unusual for her to be fifteen minutes late."

That lines up with what Connor said. While I'm sure losing Connor to prison would throw a massive wrench in the doctor's plans, there's something about his straightforward, kindly nature that makes me skeptical that he would cover for Connor purely for selfish reasons.

"Yeah, it was around that time," Meredith confirms.

"I wasn't here," Bridget offers with a shrug.

We're closing in on nine o'clock, which is when the office normally opens according to the practice's website. This style of questioning isn't getting me anywhere, anyway, – the girls might not want to open up in front of Dr. Chetty, and there might be things he doesn't feel comfortable saying in front of them. "I don't want to take up too much more of your time," I assure them, "but I was wondering if I could have a few minutes alone?"

To my surprise, Dr. Chetty nods firmly before I've had the chance to suggest we have a one-on-one. "I could spare a few minutes in my office, if that would work for you," he offers. The fact that he was so quick to jump on the idea tells me this man has something to say that I'm going to want to hear.

He turns to Meredith. "When Mrs. Altman comes in, fix her a coffee the way she likes it and let her know I'll be a few minutes."

The girls exchange a glance that could either be concern or nerves. I can't tell which. While I doubt Bridget wouldn't be much help, Meredith has been in the office since they opened. It might be worthwhile to get a few minutes with her, too.

For now, I'll follow Dr. Chetty to his office. "Dr. Lawrence's office is at the other end of the hall," he explains, pointing toward the closed oak door. "This all seems like a bad dream come to life, you know? You never imagine something like this happening in your circle. It's always somebody else."

"After having worked more cases than I can count, I can tell you that's a pretty typical reaction."

"I suppose it has to happen to somebody, right?" He holds the door open for me and I step inside. The tasteful decor is reminiscent of what I found out in the waiting room; lots of rich leather paired with wood paneled walls. These men clearly decided they wanted to project an image of prosperity, of discerning taste. I would imagine it helps their brand.

"I'm so sorry. I should've offered you something to drink. Would you like some coffee?" he asks, one hand on the doorknob, like he's ready to call out my order if I accept.

"No need. I had some this morning."

He blinks rapidly before cracking a grin. "You are either a very well-rested person or very disciplined. I don't know anybody who stops at one cup."

"Any more than that and I might get jittery."

"Fair enough. That's probably why you have such nice skin, too. You don't overdo it with the caffeine." A dermatologist said I have nice skin. I'll have to tell Mom. She'll be so proud.

He motions toward one of the two club chairs facing his desk as he walks around the long, heavy walnut desk and takes a seat behind it. "As I said, I wanted to speak privately with you over an issue. I don't think we should discuss it openly in front of the staff."

It takes everything I have not to salivate in anticipation. "Certainly."

He draws a deep breath, hesitating like he's doubting whether he should do this. I'm practically on the edge of my seat by the time he rolls his shoulders back and levels a determined gaze my way. "I happen to know for a fact my partner was having an affair."

I knew it. There had to be something. "And how do you know that?" I ask while fighting the impulse to pump my fist in the air.

He releases a heavy sigh. "Because I walked in on them."

14

ALEXIS

"Don't get me wrong." The doctor shakes his head and waves his hands. "What a man does in his personal life is his business. I have a wife and family myself, and I understand there are ebbs and flows in any marriage. Rocky phases. Challenges. It's none of my business," he says again, and I wonder if he's trying to convince himself or not.

He lowers his brow, sighing. "But when the activities take place here, on the premises, it becomes my problem as well."

I have my suspicions, but I'm going to wait. I'm not going to jump to any conclusions.

He works his forefinger under his shirt collar like it's suddenly too tight. "This is very delicate, and it pains me to air someone else's dirty laundry – especially when one of the parties is in the building at this moment."

Something tells me it wasn't Bridget. "Meredith?" I murmur.

His head bobs up and down. "At first, he swore it was a one-time thing."

"When was this, exactly?"

The man is about to turn green. I have no doubt he's asking himself whether he made the right call, opening up to me. "Three days ago."

I react before I can help myself, barking out a disbelieving, silent laugh. "Excuse me," I quickly whisper, still reeling. A day before Alyssa's disappearance? And Connor went out of his way to swear he was a faithful husband.

"I know how it sounds," the doctor groans. "And I've asked myself ever since we got word that Alyssa was missing last night whether I should say anything if the police showed up asking questions. I mean, just because a man's unfaithful doesn't mean he ..."

He cuts himself off, staring down at his desk. "I'm sure this has left you feeling awfully conflicted," I offer. My sympathy is genuine. He's trying to do the right thing, even though it makes him feel rotten.

"It's more than that," he explains. "For one thing, after I pressed him, their one-time thing turned into a six month long affair."

"They were together for six months?"

"At least. That's as much as I could get him to admit to. I made it clear I wasn't going to buy any cute little stories about getting swept off his feet or going through a midlife crisis. He's too young for that, anyway," he adds. "Finally, he broke down and spilled his guts."

"I assume you're trying to tell me they were … involved … somewhere here in the office?" It must be his kind, fatherly aura that has me tongue-tied and embarrassed.

"It was late, well past the point where we'd see any more patients that evening. I was sure they had both left for the night and that I was the only person left in the building. I walked past the first exam room, and heard them." A flush creeps up his neck. "Believe me when I tell you, I would never have opened the door if I thought I'd find them together like that. I don't know what I expected, honestly. But not that."

"Did you speak to Connor about it that evening?"

"I couldn't go home without getting some answers. Meredith hurried out, and I let him have it."

"Did he give you a reason?"

"Does anyone ever need a reason to do something like that? Really." He leans back in his chair, folding his hands over his stomach. "He's been stressed. All this time spent away from home has him on edge. Things haven't been easy lately, he and Alyssa aren't on the same page ... he went through the entire playbook from A-to-Z."

"With all due respect, I get the feeling you weren't swayed by his explanation."

"What good are those excuses in the face of the liability he opened us up to?" he counters. Now there's an edge to his voice, and I can understand why. Connor isn't the only one working long hours and making sacrifices. "Let me make one thing clear. I respect Dr. Lawrence as a dermatologist. He might not have the sort of experience I have, but he's got a way with patients. They like him, they trust him. He's also the idea man around here."

"How so?"

"He's the one with all the ideas for how to expand the business. Social media and all that." He sounds so dismissive, I'm surprised he doesn't make air quotes around the term. "I know nothing about that, or about advertising or anything. I know Alyssa offered a few ideas, as well, and he put them into practice."

"Because she worked in public relations."

"Exactly. I'm sure it's not exactly the same idea, but some of the concepts still apply. We make a good team."

"But now?"

"Now, he's left me in an impossible position. For one thing, I don't want to let Meredith go, even if she did blatantly go against the rules outlined in the employee handbook which Connor and I labored extensively over."

He rubs his temples while wearing a mournful frown. "She could very easily turn around and sue us to kingdom come, and she would have a good chance of winning the suit. Besides, she's good at her job. She's efficient, she's well liked, she has a rapport with the patients and remembers how they like their coffee when they come in. I would hate to have to start from scratch with someone else. But like I said, my hands are tied, anyway. Now, there's this general uneasiness in the air."

"Have you said anything to Meredith about this? Did you come out and have a discussion?"

"I wouldn't know where to begin." With a rueful chuckle, he adds, "I didn't turn to medicine because I'm a skilled orator, Agent Forrest. My daughters will tell you I'm about as awkward as a pig in high heels when it comes to uncomfortable discussions."

I have to press my lips together tight to hold back a smile. He seems like a very decent man, and he is completely lost on this. "I can't imagine that would be easy. I wouldn't want to be the one to broach the topic."

"He told me he would speak to her, and the following morning he said it was over. He had broken it off completely."

I wait a second before asking the obvious. "Did you believe him?"

His brows draw together. "I think I wanted to. But did I? I'm not sure of anything anymore, to tell you the truth. I'm starting to get the feeling he told me what he knew I'd want to hear, and that's all. It's enough to make me wonder about a lot of things."

I feel sorry for him, genuinely sorry. He's a man who's been put in an awful position by someone who he was supposed to be able to trust. "It's almost like you have a marriage of your own, the two of you," I muse. "You have to be able to trust each other with everything, or else …"

"It all falls apart," he finishes for me before nodding his head. "That's right. That's exactly right. And all it takes is one lie to make you question everything else. I'm babbling," he suddenly announces. "And I do have a patient who'll be waiting for me. I'm sure you have plenty of work, as well. I'm sorry to have taken up so much of your time."

Sorry? The man is a gold mine. I would never be crass enough to announce that out loud, but that's what he is. He has confirmed my suspicions, for one thing. There's no reason for Connor to come out and announce what a faithful, good boy he was before the question left my lips. He was a little too adamant. Too descriptive. Like a child overdoing it while trying to cover up a lie.

"I have to ask you this." He crosses the room but rather than open the door for me, he stands with his back to it. "Are you going to question Meredith next?"

"I'm going to have to. But don't worry," I continue when pain pinches his features. "I won't do it here. We'll be offsite, I promise."

"Thank you very much." I can practically feel his relief. "The last thing we need is a scandal like this getting out in the open. You'd be surprised how quickly news can spread."

All I can do is laugh gently. "I grew up in Broken Hill. Believe me. I know all too well how little it takes for a story to get out of hand. I'll be discreet."

"Thank you so much. And ..." He clears his throat awkwardly as he opens the door. "Really, I hope she's found soon."

I have to do it. I need to know. "Do you think your partner has it in him to harm his wife?" I whisper.

If only he didn't hesitate before shaking his head. "No. No, he could never. He doesn't have it in him. He loves those kids too much – that, I believe."

I have to wonder if he's telling himself that because he needs to believe it. Because that's what he needs to tell himself.

Meredith makes no pretense of having been busy when she spots me stepping through the door leading back out to the waiting area. "Is there anything else you need help with, detective?" she asks. I notice the middle-aged woman seated close to the desk who sits up a little straighter and stops flipping through the magazine in her lap.

I turned my back to her, facing Meredith with a smile. "I'm not a detective," I remind her gently. "I'm a Special Agent with the FBI. I don't think any of the police around here would appreciate hearing you call me a detective. It's bad enough some of them don't like the FBI meddling in their business."

"Oh, sure. I'm sorry." This girl is anxious. She keeps twisting a strand of hair around one finger, and her chair emits a high-pitched squeak every time her knee jogs up and down. The sound would drive me crazy if I had to work all day with her.

"It's not a problem. Listen," I whisper, leaning in. "Are you free to grab a coffee or some lunch later today? I would like to speak with you, but offsite. Would that work? My treat."

If she sinks her teeth any deeper into her lip, she's going to draw blood. Just like Dr. Chetty, she's torn, conflicted. Wondering if it would be unfaithful to Connor if she speaks privately with me. "Sure," she decides. "Bridget could fill in for me at the desk for fifteen or twenty minutes. There is a coffee shop across the road."

"I'm familiar with it," I tell her, envisioning the quaint little shop. It's positioned perfectly, considering there's a busy office park within walking distance. They must make a killing.

"I can meet you there …" She glances at her computer screen. "Ten-thirty?"

"I'll be there."

Now, all I can do is hope she doesn't call Connor before then, so he'll have the chance to coach her.

15

ALEXIS

It's nearly ten-thirty and I'm sitting at a table by the window looking out toward the business park. *Please, don't leave me hanging.* I don't think she will, and it's not as if I couldn't find her if she stands me up. I would rather not have to actively pursue her, is all. I don't want to escalate things unless it's absolutely necessary. Right now, that doesn't seem to be the case, but if she leaves me hanging, it might be a different story.

There are a handful of people sitting around me. A couple of them type on keyboards, while the others enjoy a late breakfast over a book or while having a conversation with a friend. It's warm and cozy, in stark contrast to the increasingly miserable weather outside. The morning started cloudy, and now a thin, icy rain falls. The sort of day when all a person wants to do is curl up under a blanket, preferably beside a cuddle partner.

The thought of Mitch stirs my lips into a smile. He knocked it out of the park last night at Mom's. And Mom, for her part, behaved well. Even mentioning Maddie didn't seem to be enough to permanently ruin the mood.

It's closing in on ten-thirty and there's still no sign of Meredith. She's probably nervous, questioning whether it's a good idea to sit down with me. Whether it would mean being unfaithful to her boyfriend. Normally, I would record an interview like this, and I would make sure the other party knows they're being recorded. Yet for some reason, the idea of announcing it makes my skin prickle and my doubts flare to life. She might be less likely to open up if this seems like an official interview, and the entire reason I chose to meet up this way rather than having her come to the station is to keep her feeling relaxed and easy.

Well, Maine is a one party consent state. I don't need to announce anything. Granted, if she tells me something significant, the sort of thing that could break the case wide open, I might not be able to use it. But that's a chance I'm going to have to take. I want to be sure I keep everything straight – her version of events, Dr. Chetty's, Connor's.

A flash of movement nearby catches my eye, and I look up to find Meredith hurrying across the slick parking lot. She's still in her patent leather stilettos, and she must be freezing in her jean skirt. I've never been the sort of girl willing to sacrifice comfort for fashion, and I admire women like her. Though really, she could've chosen a safer pair of shoes – she slips twice before reaching the door and almost hurling herself into the shop.

I raise a hand to get her attention and she nods in recognition before going to the counter to order a drink. So much for this being my treat, I guess. Did she speak to Connor? I won't know until I know. If her attitude changes, if she seems withholding or nervous, I'll know what I'm dealing with.

"Hi." She joins me after another couple of minutes, lowering the hood of her coat and carefully running her fingers through her hair. She still looks fantastic. She must've touched up her makeup before leaving, since her lips are freshly glossed.

"Thank you for taking a few minutes to sit with me. How are things over there?"

"We've gotten a few phone calls asking about Dr. Lawrence." She holds the cup between her trembling hands and blows across the surface of her latte before taking a sip.

"Concern, or gossip?"

Her lips twitch, but that's pretty much the only part of her face that moves. "Gossip disguised as concern?"

Smart girl. "I wanted to speak to you one on one since I don't know anybody who would be completely upfront and open when their boss is in the room. I didn't want to put you in that position."

"No, it's okay. I understand. But really, I don't have any complaints. It's a great place to work."

She lowers her gaze to her drink and her very white, even teeth sink into her bottom lip while her chest rises and falls in a deep breath. "I'm just going to say it. Connor and I have been having an affair. I'm not trying to waste my time or yours, so I'm going to put it out there."

"I appreciate that."

"Don't tell me you didn't already know." She glances up at me. "I figured Dr. Chetty told you all about it right away. When you were in his office."

"It could be pertinent information."

"But I swear." Her eyes shine with an almost intense light. She's unblinking, demanding I believe her. "I don't have the first clue what happened to Alyssa. I don't know where she could be or why she went missing. I had nothing to do with any of this."

"Let's take it back a little bit and start from the beginning," I suggest. Folding my arms on the table, I lean in. "How long have the two of you been involved?"

"Since not long after I started working with him. Almost a year now."

Which is twice as long as Connor insisted to Dr. Chetty. Does this man have the vaguest idea of the meaning of truth? Or is the truth whatever happens to suit him at the moment?

"So you know him pretty well now, I would guess." Her head bobs up and down. "Do you think Connor has it in him to hurt his wife?"

"Absolutely not," her voice is flat and firm. "That's not who he is. He might not be the best husband, but he is not a violent man. And I know he would never, ever do anything to hurt the kids. They're his world—I know it sounds like a cliché, but it's the truth. He adores them, and it would break their hearts if Alyssa were hurt or … worse." Again, the only hint of an expression comes in the form of a chewed lip. The rest of her face hardly moves.

"I mean," she continues, "they were having their issues. But he was going to do things the right way."

"Meaning what?"

"Meaning he was going to break up with her. He wasn't going to kill her."

Now I wish I had a face full of Botox so I could conceal my surprise. It's helpful during an interview to remain as neutral as possible, but a bombshell like that makes neutrality a challenge. "Please, elaborate. They were going to split up?"

She heaves a sigh before sipping her drink, leaving me hanging. There's at least one thing I'm fairly sure of, she has not spoken to Connor today. I can only imagine he would tell her to not under any circumstances admit to anything this incriminating.

"That was why he wasn't into the whole IVF thing," she explains. "He didn't want to have another kid with her, because he knew it was over. He's known for a long time."

"And did she know he felt this way?"

"I don't know," she admits. "But I mean, it's not like she was happy, either. I didn't tell him this because it's not my place, but I got the feeling she was trying to use another baby as a way to bring them back together. I've had friends who've done that. It never works out."

"Yes, that's one of the oldest stories in the book," I agree, drawing her out. "It's not fair to the kid."

"Right?" She rolls her eyes and clicks her tongue, but then she would, wouldn't she? She can afford to roll her eyes at the silly wife of the man she's been sleeping with for almost a year. It's very easy for the other woman to be disdainful.

"Have you two made any plans?" I prompt. "I mean real, solid plans? Or was this all a bunch of talk?"

"Oh, no, we definitely have been making plans." Her eyes go wide. "I've been looking at apartments for us and everything. And I was going to break up with my boyfriend soon – maybe this week, maybe next."

She has a boyfriend? I can barely keep up with the information she's dropping on me. I wonder how she can be so blasé. Discussing the plans to break up with her boyfriend the way she might talk about an appointment at the salon.

"Connor knew you were going to do this?"

"We just talked about it a couple of days ago, the day before Alyssa went missing." She closes her eyes and releases a shuddering breath. "I know it sounds awful. It's so messed up. But I'm telling you, he couldn't have had anything to do with this. He was so worried when he was leaving the office after that call came in that the kids needed to be picked up. He was really worried. I know him. I can tell."

That doesn't mean much, unfortunately. I'm sure Alyssa felt she knew her husband, as well.

The fact that I thought of her in the past tense isn't a good sign, either.

16

KILLER

She's leaving now. The girl she's with stands and buttons her coat, then lifts her hood. Wouldn't want to get her pretty hair wet in the rain. I've never understood what men see in women like her. Sure, there's a nice outer shell, but it's all for show. Everything planned, everything polished to the hilt. No warmth, no authenticity.

I suppose that's why I've always been drawn to younger people. I don't have much patience for phonies, and that's what this girl screams without having to say a word. I'm phony. Everything about me is an illusion.

A sudden, startled laugh bubbles out of me as I sit in my truck, parked a few spots down from the Corolla belonging to my favorite person. Maybe I have more in common with that overly made up girl than I imagined. I know what it's like to wear a mask. I would never have gotten as far as I have for as long as I have without the ability to blend in and disguise my true nature.

Whoever that girl is, she's made Alexis happy. My spirits lift when I see the small, satisfied smile Alexis wears upon exiting the coffee shop. What is she going to do now? Return to the station and share the good news? Does she go home to celebrate with Mom? Or will she flee to the bookstore and that bland boyfriend of hers?

My hands tighten around the wheel in anticipation, and once she's pulled back out of her spot and turned towards the road, I start my engine and fall in behind her. As usual, she's too absorbed by whatever is on her mind to notice my pursuit. Once we reach Main Street after ten minutes of driving, she slows down considerably, and I realize once she hits the brakes that she's looking for a parking spot. There's a car pulling out half a block down from where I am sitting at a red light – I hang a right turn when I spot an open space nearby and park around the corner from where Alexis does.

Does she understand this thrill? Certainly, she devotes much of her life to pursuing criminals, but has she ever stalked them? Become intimately aware of their routine? Has she ever placed herself in their lives?

I wait around the corner of the building at the end of the block, an old bank that was converted to a boutique shop. I doubt she's around to do any shopping today. When eleven-thirty rolls around and Mitch Dutton comes strolling down the block, I can't help but snicker. What she sees in him, I have no idea.

Yet she wastes no time, almost throwing her door open and hurrying around the car, taking his hand once he reaches her. The smile they share makes me wrinkle my nose, but I manage to maintain my composure. Honestly, he's nothing. No one. But there's no accounting for taste.

I wait a minute after they've walked hand-in-hand into a sandwich shop two doors down from where I stand. By the time I meander my way over there, several other customers have ducked inside to escape the rain. We're coming up on the lunch hour, and the shop is bustling by the time I enter and get in line. There are five customers between me and the happy couple. While I watch, Alexis stands on tiptoe and brushes her lips against Mitch's cheek, then whispers something in his ear that makes him laugh.

What a perfect little couple they are. High school sweethearts reunited. Agent Forrest isn't the only one in town who knows how to do research or how to listen when people gossip. I've made it my business to visit the bookstore a couple of times a week to get a better feel for who he is and what they are together.

And still, she doesn't know. Is it arrogance, or is it simply a matter of ignorance? Of all people, she should know how easy it is to overlook the obvious. How wickedness can exist alongside goodness.

Once they order and pay, they step out of line and snag a table by the window overlooking the street. It was recently vacated, and Mitch goes through the motions of wiping the table down with a paper napkin before Alexis takes a seat across from him. What a gentleman.

"What can I get for you?" I didn't realize I'd reached the front of the line until the girl behind the register chirped in her cheerful little voice. Too busy observing.

I do a quick glance over the menu on the board behind the girl's head. "I'll try your Philly cheesesteak," I reply, admiring the sparkly barrettes she wears in her copper hair while she enters my order into the system. "I've spent time in Philadelphia. Let's see what your idea of an authentic steak looks like." She offers a weak smile to go with my receipt.

It's my lucky day. It just so happens that while I'm waiting for my sandwich, the table beside Alexis and Mitch opens up. I snag it before anyone else can, taking a seat and practically biting my tongue off to hold back gleeful laughter. Now this is meant to be. I enjoy it when fate steps in like this. I take my seat and wait to hear the name Bob called out, as that's the name I gave when I ordered. I need to pay attention, or else it will look pretty strange when I don't answer.

Someone calls out for Mitch and he pops up from the table, brushing against the sleeve of my puffy jacket on his way to the counter. He reeks of some overpowering cologne that turns my stomach. There are definite benefits to possessing an excellent sense of smell, but then there are downsides as well. I want to gag at the cloying stench.

Alexis, on the other hand, doesn't bother with things like that. Every time I've gotten close to her, I've picked up nothing but the faint scent of soap. Because she doesn't need all those things to cover up who she is. Even then, I have to get very close to pick up the faintest whiff.

Right now, I don't smell anything coming from her table. I'm so close. my heart flutters like the wings of a hummingbird and I can barely contain my glee. Alexis is busy scrolling through her phone, frowning as she reads something or other. She wouldn't be frowning if I announced myself, would she? *Soon, soon.* The thought gives me immense pleasure.

I wonder what sort of boyfriend Madeline would have chosen for herself. A smart girl like her? I have no doubt she would choose someone with a little more potential than the town's bookstore owner. I suppose compared to her jailbird father, Mitch looks like a real prize.

"Bob! Cheesesteak for Bob!" I don't hesitate when I hear my alias called out, and I rise from my chair to grab the sandwich. Green peppers. Why do people always think green peppers belong on a cheesesteak? I take a seat, then take a bite. At least the quality of the meat is good, and I appreciate the use of provolone. Even so, there's very little authenticity about this. Something tells me they don't care, but I've always believed words matter.

"I wish I could say it got me anywhere." Alexis sounds mournful, picking at a chicken salad sandwich.

"Your interview?" Mitch asks. What else could she be talking about? For someone who is around books all day, he's not very quick on the uptake. He could never get away with the sort of activities I've enjoyed for so many years.

"I need to find a way to get a confession, but I still don't have anything solid to use as leverage." Alexis sighs, rolling her head from side to side. "Anyway, how are you? How has your morning been?"

I watch from the corner of my eye, and something hot and bitter fills my throat when I catch the way she smiles at him. The light in her eyes, the softness that takes over her delicate features. Features so much like her sister's, it's uncanny. Strange how there are so many names and faces and locations that have faded until they're little more than ghosts in the back of my consciousness, but Madeline comes through strong and clear. She left an impression on me, putting it mildly. I wish her sister could understand that. What it meant to have that beautiful, wise soul with me for so long. Knowing it was dangerous, yet unable to let her go.

The way I can't let go of Alexis. It's a good thing I've learned to blend in, or there would be no hope of coming this close to her unnoticed. And there's no way I could stop. I've already tried.

"I think I'm going to have to bring the husband back in," Alexis decides. "This time, put the screws to him and hope he cracks. The kids deserve closure someday, at least."

It's boring, really, the way the cops always focus on the husband in cases such as this. Sure, the husband might be responsible in ninety percent of missing person cases.

But there's always the other ten percent, isn't there?

17

ALEXIS

"Please, tell me you found something. Tell me that's why you brought me here again."

All things considered, Connor Lawrence has no business adopting this sort of attitude when we meet in the interrogation room at the station. Clearly, he feels differently than he did when he was here the day of his wife's disappearance.

I take my time, sitting down with the notes I've transcribed from my interview with Meredith and the impressions I took from my conversation with Dr. Chetty. "There was something you said to me at your house that stood out, Dr. Lawrence. I was wondering if you could provide further insight."

"Insight into what?" He folds his hands on the table, sitting up straight and tall, meeting my gaze without blinking or flinching. He doesn't look so much like the grieving spouse anymore, nor is he the scattered dad worried for his kids. He's taking it personally, the fact that I've brought him back in. So much for wanting to do everything in his power to help.

Clearly, he senses my interest in him as a suspect. I guess it wouldn't make me feel very comfortable, either.

"You volunteered information without my asking. Let me see … what exactly did you say …" I flip through my notes, taking more time than necessary. Drawing it out, letting him sweat a little. "Oh, right. I said I was about to ask you something, and you cut me off by assuring me you were not having an affair. You had never been anything but faithful to your wife, and there wasn't anything close to a flirtation with your receptionist."

I look up from my notes to find his brows drawing together and his jaw tightening. "Do you remember saying this?" I ask.

"I'm sure I did." The confidence in his voice is almost admirable.

"Were you telling me the truth, Dr. Lawrence?"

"I don't see what this has to do with my wife's disappearance."

Way to avoid the question. "Are you sure about that?" Forget the kid gloves. It's time to get serious.

It's clear he's surprised considering the way his head snaps back before he scowls. "Why don't you try telling me what this is really all about? Have you found anything about Alyssa? Or are you too busy interrogating innocent people to do the job of finding my wife?"

"Interesting how you're suddenly so concerned about your wife," I counter. "From what I understand, you haven't always been so concerned over her welfare."

"What is that supposed to mean?"

"Loving, faithful husbands don't carry on with their employees."

Hatred. That's the only word for what twists his handsome face into something nasty. "That is an ugly, baseless accusation."

"Dr. Lawrence, let's be real with each other, shall we?" I've had about as much as I can stand of his self-righteous act. Does he think I'm making this up? That there's no basis to my insinuations? Maybe. Maybe he thinks I'm throwing darts at a wall, hoping something will stick.

Tapping a pen to my notebook, I drop the bombshell. "I visited your office."

He draws a sharp breath. His lips pull back from his teeth in an expression of dismay, maybe horror. He wasn't counting on his partner sharing secrets. "Who did you talk to? What did they say?"

"I think you know the answer to both of those questions, sir. This will go a lot easier if you simply tell the truth. The full truth. Not the version you think will be easiest for me to swallow."

He folds his arms, leaning back in the chair, and his gaze is shrewd. He looks me up and down like he's finally seeing me for the first time. Finally understanding this isn't a game, and he's not nearly as clever as he believes himself to be.

It's like we're playing a game of chess, and he's trying to decipher my next move before making one of his own. "Fine," he eventually grunts. "It's true. I've been having an affair with Meredith."

"Thank you for finally being honest," I murmur. "And that does line up with what she offered."

He nods slowly, chuckling without humor. "I'm sure she told you everything. She has a different idea about what our relationship is and where it's going."

"With all due respect, I'm going to have to take what you say with a grain of salt. According to Dr. Chetty, the two of you had only been together for six months. According to Meredith, it's been closer to the entirety of your practice's existence. It seems like you have a habit of telling people whatever it is you think they need to hear, the way you told me you've never so much as flirted with your receptionist. Considering the fact your partner found the two of you together the night before Alyssa disappeared, I'd say you've done a lot more than flirt with her."

Finally, the facade cracks and his panic pours through. "This has nothing to do with Alyssa! What do I have to say to get that through your head? You're wasting time worrying about something that's completely inconsequential."

"That's not for you to say. In a case like this, when a woman goes missing and we find out her husband's been having an affair for a year with a woman he planned to move in with —"

"What?" He barks out a laugh. "She told you that? Of course, she would. And that's what I'm talking about when I say we had a different idea of the way our relationship was going."

This man has more excuses than anyone I've ever interviewed, and that's saying something. "Then why don't you explain to me how you saw your relationship going?"

He doesn't hesitate. "Nowhere. It was going nowhere."

"That's news to me. And something tells me it would be news to Meredith, too."

"I know." He drops his arms to his sides and looks rather helpless, but that could be an act, too. I'm sure he has plenty of faces, masks he changes at will. It all depends on the situation and who he's dealing with.

"I'm guessing you hadn't shared this opinion with Meredith."

He squirms under my gaze. It's something I would have sat down with Meredith over if it hadn't been for Alyssa disappearing. My partner found us together the night before that."

"I know."

He flinches but quickly recovers. "Yeah, I guess he would have told you. He's a decent man. He always wants to do what's right. I can't hold it against him – it was my stupid fault for doing that in the office, anyway. There's no one but myself to blame."

He's not going to get an argument out of me. He is also not going to get any sympathy.

"I did a lot of thinking that night, after I left the office. Really, I know it's easy for me to say that now, but it's the truth. Talking with Stuart shined a new light on everything. He reminded me of what matters. What we're building this practice for. Not for ourselves, but for our families. And the more I thought about it, the more obvious it was that he was right. I was selfish and stupid to get involved with that girl. It was just one of those things."

He slides a guilty look my way and frowns when he finds no warmth on this side of the table. I certainly hope he doesn't expect me to sympathize with him.

"Look. I've known for a while I had to break it off. But getting found out and getting lectured was the last straw."

"You knew for a while?" I counter. "Because according to Meredith, you were looking for an apartment together."

"No." The force behind that word, those two little letters, takes me by surprise. "Absolutely not. That was all her idea. She was looking for a place, not me. And it was when she started talking along those lines that I knew I had to end things. I have no interest in leaving my wife and children. Things between me and Alyssa have been strained – which you know – and that resulted in a lot less intimacy. Meredith filled a need. That's all. But aside from the physical aspects of our relationship, we're completely incompatible. We would never work."

That wasn't enough to convince him to stop sleeping with her, was it? Not until somebody older and wiser lectured him.

Leaning forward, his face crumples like a used tissue with emotion that may or may not be authentic. I'm not sure. "Agent Forrest. I'm sure you've heard this before, but you've got to believe me. I love Alyssa. Yes, we are having issues, but that happens in just about every marriage at some point or another. That doesn't mean I wanted to leave her, or that I wanted to get her out of the way, or anything else like that. Our children need her. I need her. And she could still be out there somewhere, needing us, while you and I sit here and discuss my infidelity."

His eyes filled with tears which he rubs away with his knuckles. "I swear, when I get her back, I'm going to be the husband she deserves. Whatever she needs, whatever she wants, she's got it. We're going to start over. I have to believe we can start over."

All I can do is sit and watch as he slowly crumbles.

And once again, I wonder if anyone is capable of faking that kind of emotion so believably.

18

ALYSSA

"**O**h. I know that look."

I'll freeze in the act of entering the captain's office, cocking my head at his announcement. "Come again?"

"The way you look right now. You're disappointed, aren't you?"

Disappointed is one word for it. I'm also more conflicted than ever, not to mention frustrated. That's the one I go with. "It's not that I expected him to come out with a confession, but why does he have to seem so genuine?"

"Are you losing confidence?"

"That we'll eventually find out what happened to her? Not at all." I sink into a chair, rubbing my hands along my thighs to vent some of the energy bubbling away in me. That woman is still out there somewhere, and we don't have the first idea where she is. "But I am losing confidence that we're going to find her in time to help her. I'm losing confidence that we never had a chance."

He sits across from me, and I notice the crumpled fast food wrappers spilling from his wastebasket. "When was the last time you had a home-cooked meal?" I ask.

He doesn't seem surprised by the question. "When was the last time we didn't have a missing woman on our hands? Not just a missing woman, but a young mother? The press are insatiable. I had a young woman ask me point-blank when I stopped at the gas station whether we were going to get off our butts and find Alyssa."

His mouth draws into a thin, disapproving line. "And she didn't use the word butts exactly."

"You watched the interview. Did you get a feeling about him?"

"I think he's slimy." It's rare for him to come straight out and offer such a strong opinion in such a no-nonsense manner. "And I think he's finally coming to realize where all of his double talk and empty promises got him. He's a man who dug a deep hole for himself."

"Do you think he's a killer?" Because let's face it, that's more than likely what we are dealing with now. Every inch of the area Alyssa Lawrence typically ran has been combed over multiple times for any signs of her. Her wedding ring, her hair scrunchie, any little piece of her. So far, nothing.

He takes a deep breath, then shakes his head the way I knew he would. "You met with the girl he was having the affair with. What did you think about her?"

"How so, in what way?"

"Whose version of the story is the truth? The way she makes it sound, they were in the middle of a serious relationship that was about to take the next step. Is he telling the truth, or is she?"

"Considering his track record with the truth, I'm inclined to believe her," I admit. "Granted, she wouldn't be the first young woman who let her imagination run away with her when it came to a relationship. She might have thought they were a lot more serious than they were. She could have been the one pushing to move in together."

"Or, it could've been him," the captain concludes. "Clearly, he wouldn't want to tell us about that now. He has to know how incriminating this is. Of course, it would lead us to ask questions. Did Alyssa know? Was she planning on taking the kids from him?"

"But that would contradict her determination to have another baby," I point out. It's like trying to navigate a spiderweb.

"She might have found out very recently, shortly before she disappeared. For all we know," he points out with a tired sigh, "Dr. Chetty could've called her that night. She might have known by the time Connor got home that he was involved with Meredith. Considering all of this happened the night before she disappeared, it doesn't look good."

The way he lays it out, the case is practically solved. Wife finds out her husband is being unfaithful. Wife has already sacrificed her career, her aspirations, everything for the sake of being a wife and mother. By all appearances, the perfect wife and mother. The perfect home, the perfect life. It doesn't take much conjecture to imagine her confronting him.

But would he have waited until the following morning to get rid of her? I feel myself deflating once that point works its way into my head. "If anything happened that night — a big fight, a blowup, something that would've made him lose his temper and do the unthinkable — it would have been one thing. Inexcusable, but at least slightly understandable. It's happened thousands of times."

"But we know that didn't happen, since Alyssa dropped the kids off the next morning."

"And there was that friend of hers," I recall, going through my notes. "She saw her that morning, invited her for coffee. I get the feeling that if there were so much as a hair out of place on that woman's head, Elizabeth Currid would have noticed. She already has pretty strong opinions of Connor. She would have told me about it."

"We can rule that out – still, they could have argued. She could have told him to take his things and go. Anything could've happened."

That's just it. Anything could have happened. Who to believe? "I'm curious about this Meredith."

"How so?"

"According to her, she was ready to dump her boyfriend and move in with Connor. What if she got tired of waiting for Connor to make up his mind and break things off with Alyssa?"

He lifts his brows, lips pursed as he thinks this over. "That's an interesting theory. Does she seem the type?"

"Is there a type when it comes to this kind of thing? She is in love – at least, she thinks she is. She's serious enough about Connor to break off a relationship for him. Looking for apartments, probably envisioning herself as a doctor's wife someday."

"But she was in the office at the time Alyssa went on her run," he reminds me. "Just like Connor was."

"And the girl who works part-time wasn't in, so she couldn't pop out for a coffee date that turned into something else," I recall. "But it is possible there was some time between appointments. Or maybe she had help? Maybe they met up at Meredith's request? Maybe Alyssa knew what was up and called to see if Meredith could meet up?"

"It all seems possible. Right now, it looks like both Connor and Meredith are suspects." We exchange a look, and I know he's thinking what I'm thinking. There's a lot more work ahead of us.

"Let's find Meredith's friends," he decides. "Connor's friends, as well. Let's find out if Meredith talked to anybody, gave them an idea she was ready to take the next steps with Connor, if she had any frustrations with him dragging his feet, that type of thing. Does she seem like someone who would gossip with her girlfriends?"

"Definitely." It takes no consideration to come to that conclusion. I can easily imagine her sitting at brunch with the girls, talking about how great it would be if only her boyfriend's wife wasn't in the way.

"We can start there, try to build a case against Meredith if we can. We might also look into whether Alyssa was socking money away."

"Like if she was preparing to run off with the kids?"

"Right. Did she have separate bank accounts? Credit cards? There has to be a trail somewhere. We just haven't found it yet."

We just haven't found anything yet. That's the problem. Days later, all we have to go on is speculation. Theories. Thin ones, at that. I'm in the dark, flailing around, trying to find a light switch.

"She couldn't have vanished into thin air." I don't know if I'm trying to convince myself or simply stating a fact. "It's not possible."

"Tell that to all the people who've never been found. Decades later, all over the world, there are people wondering what happened to their loved one."

There have been times I've asked myself what it would've been like if Maddie had never been found. At least we have closure – a mantra my mother adopted and held close to her heart. As terrible as things were, it would have been infinitely worse if the question of what ever happened to my sister hung over us.

19

ALEXIS

It's still raining when I leave the station, having decided to do another drive around Alyssa's neighborhood and see if there's anyone who has remembered anything that didn't come to mind the day of her disappearance. Sometimes, it takes a while for memories to bubble to the surface. Situations and conversations which might not have seemed very important in the moment tend to get tucked away deep in a person's memory.

It's still just as miserable outside, bleak, and my breath immediately forms a heavy cloud that's driven away by the raindrops. The rain is determined to drive the cold into my bones – right away, it soaks into my coat and weighs it down. That could also be my frustration weighing on me.

I hate to think of Alyssa being out here somewhere in this. I hate to think of those kids wondering where their mom is. They're too young to understand what's happening now, but eventually they're going to clue into her absence. They'll want to know why she never came home.

I would like to know why, too. Something about this entire situation does not sit right with me, even more so than the average missing persons case. It's the vanishing-into-thin-air aspect. A day or two, fine, but it's been far too long now. Too long for there to be no sign of her.

Whoever did this had to plan it. This was not some crime of convenience, an accidental crossing of paths. It was calculated. This woman was removed from her own life, like a puzzle piece plucked away from the ones around her.

I'm mulling this over as I reach my car, grumbling to myself over the dead ends I keep hitting and the prospect of navigating rain slick roads for the rest of the afternoon. I'm so deep in my aggravation, I almost miss the slip of paper tucked under my windshield. It's not a ticket – though the idea makes my lips stir in the closest thing to a smile I've worn in hours. Getting a ticket while parked in the station lot.

It's just like Mitch to leave a note like this for me to find when I come outside, though the rain has ruined it somewhat. I carefully unfold the paper to make sure it stays in one piece, smiling in anticipation. We only had lunch a few hours ago, but it's not like I can never get enough of him.

Immediately, all thoughts of Mitch are dispelled when I read the message, printed in block letters using black ink.

You've gotten close. Closer than you think.

But you'll never catch me.

But I might decide to find you one day.

My mouth goes dry and a sick feeling washes over me as I scan the lines again. The note trembles in my hands before my head snaps up, swinging wildly in all directions as I try to locate the person who left this. It's not very wet, telling me it hasn't been here for long. He could be nearby. He could be behind me this very second.

I spin on my heel, ready to confront him. Ready to draw my gun if need be because if this was written by the man who killed my sister and all those other kids, he's not a man to underestimate.

Is this it? Is it him? Or is it a prank?

A few raindrops hit the note and right away I fold it back up and hold it in my closed hand to protect it from any further damage. Where is he? He has to be nearby.

He knows my car. He's been following me. He knows where to find me, which means he could know where I live. He could know everything about me.

Enough. I can almost hear the word reverberating in my head, as sharp and as loud as a gunshot. I've given myself a moment to panic, and that's as much as I can afford. Now it's time to pull it together and take the next steps.

And I thought it felt bleak out here before this? Now the bare trees that sway in the cold wind seem to watch me. They're an ominous reminder that I am never truly alone. If only they could tell me who did this and where they went.

Reason finally kicks in. I'm holding this note in my bare hand, getting my fingerprints all over it. What I need to do is get it to the lab immediately for processing. I run back into the station, then unfold the note again once I'm inside and it's protected from the rain. Now I hold it by the corners using my nails.

It's written on the back of a CVS receipt. Sure, why not? Stop off at the drugstore, grab a few things, write a threatening message. No doubt that's just another day in the life of a psychotic murderer.

Andy Cobb notices me and lets out a sharp whistle. "Thought you were leaving. You just can't get enough of this place, can you?"

His goofy grin fades when he sees my face. "I need an evidence bag," I reply as I rush toward him.

He's quick to find one and hold it open for me so I can slide the note inside. "What is this?"

"I'm still not sure." I place the bag on his desk and take a picture of both sides of the note before snatching it up. "I found it on my windshield."

"You all right?" For once, he's not offering some sarcastic quip.

I don't have time to get into it. All I can do is shrug – because seriously, I don't know if I'm all right – before dashing downstairs to where the crime scene investigator offices are located.

"I need you to FedEx this to the CSI lab in Virginia immediately." My hand is still trembling when I hand the bag over to the first person I find. She must see my wide-eyed stare and interpret it correctly, since she wastes no time asking questions.

"On it," she assures me, then pulls out a FedEx envelope and begins assembling the package.

All that's left now is to question every single aspect of my life. Here I was, thinking I was following him. Looking into his past, his connections, his habits.

All the time, he's been watching me. Now I wonder how long it's been since he started tracking me. How much of my life has he been privy to?

Was he watching from somewhere nearby, waiting for me to find his message? I can't fight off the trembling that overwhelms me any more than I can keep from imagining the implications behind a single note.

20

ALEXIS

"**A**lexis? What are you still doing here?"

Captain Felch's voice penetrates the fog that's wrapped itself around my brain. No, it's worse than a fog, come to think of it. It's a blanket. Thick and heavy enough that it makes keeping my head up a chore. I want to lie down. I want to think.

Not that it would make a difference.

"Alexis." He steps into my makeshift office and stands beside my chair, his hand dropping onto my shoulder. That's what snaps me out of my blank shock.

I look up at him, blinking fast. "I'm sorry," I murmur. My mouth is parched and my lip stings from the chewing I've done. "I was waiting here."

"Waiting for what? You told me you were going to ride around Alyssa's neighborhood. That was more than an hour ago – have you been here all this time?"

I nod when my voice fails me. How long has he been watching? Where is he now? Is it him, really him? "I'm waiting."

"So you told me." He leans on the desk, gazing down at me in obvious concern. "What are you waiting for?"

I need to pull myself together. The only feeling I can compare this to is waking up from a long afternoon nap, fuzzy and wondering what day it is. Sitting up straighter, I square my shoulders. "Confirmation. One of the girls downstairs put a package together for me and sent it to the lab in Virginia. I had her expedite it. I called the lab and let them know it was on its way. I'm waiting for confirmation the package got picked up." And thinking. Wondering. Looking back on the past days and weeks, asking myself whether he was watching.

"What did you send? You found something new?"

Alexis, get it together. A glance at the clock tells me I have, indeed, been sitting here for more than an hour as the world has kept turning around me. Sitting and questioning.

My phone is sitting on the desk. I turn it over and pull up the photos I took earlier. Handing it to him, I explain, "I found this on my car when I went outside. I've never left the station."

He tips his head to the side, studying the image. "I don't understand. Someone left this for you?"

"Under my wiper. It was waiting for me when I went outside. Like I said, I sent it to the lab for analysis, then I guess I sort of zoned out."

"Oh, no." He goes back-and-forth between the two images, the front and back of the note. "Any idea who might've left it?"

"You have to know where my mind immediately went."

His eyes meet mine before going narrow, his brows drawing together over the bridge of his slightly crooked nose. "You think so? Do you think he's been in town all this time?" It's almost a relief, really, that I don't have to explain myself.

"All this time? I'm not sure. Right now?" I shrug when words fail me. "I've sat here all this time, going back over everything I've done over the last week or more. Everywhere I've gone, everyone I've seen, spoken to. Was he there?"

"It could have been anyone," he reminds me. I can tell he's doing his best to reassure me, but he doesn't believe himself. He might hope, but he doesn't believe it.

"Who am I most actively involved in searching for?" I counter. "There's only one person it could be."

"If it is him," he points out as he hands the phone back, "it means you're getting close."

He makes a point. Somehow, it doesn't help me feel any better. "It also means I'm not half as good at my job as I think I am, if he's been able to identify me and he knows I'm searching for him."

"He's bound to know you're searching for him. You headed up Camille and Lila's cases. You met him at the Academy, albeit briefly. He knew why you were there."

"No doubt he could have gotten my name from the visitor logs," I realize, and the realization hits me hard. All this time I've been imagining him running away in fear, flying away like a scared rabbit who knows the hunter has picked up his presence. This is not my first case. I didn't graduate from my Bureau training yesterday.

Yet it didn't occur to me that he would turn the tables and learn more about me.

"If it's him," I whisper, "does that mean he knows about the connection? Maddie?"

He releases a sigh that speaks volumes before he says a word. "It could be."

"You're going out of your way to be kind about this," I point out with a brief but appreciative grin.

"I don't want to jump to any conclusions. It is possible he made the connection between you and your sister." He holds up a finger, narrowing his gaze. "There's another side to this. It's been twenty years since Maddie died. It could be he never made the connection and is only interested in you because he knows you're on to him."

But how do I feel? What is my gut telling me? It's been screaming the same thing since I took the time to sit down and process everything. He knows. He knows and that knowledge makes all of this so much more delicious and enjoyable for him.

"Let's look at this from another angle." He taps the phone with one finger. "What can we tell based off of the evidence?"

"For one thing, that CVS is still printing out mile-long receipts with every purchase."

He snorts at my pitiful attempt at a joke. "Yes, that is pretty wasteful. Where is the store located? Is there an address printed on the receipt?"

I pull up the picture and expand it, zooming in. "Yes. It's the one in town, out by the strip mall. Not ten minutes away."

"And when was the receipt printed?"

Taking a look, I report, "A few hours ago."

"So he stopped at the pharmacy, got his receipt, decided to write you a note."

I take his theory and let it play out in my mind's eye. Something about it doesn't sit right. "He wouldn't do that," I decide, shaking my head.

"Why is that?"

"It would be sloppy." It seems obvious to me, yet he still looks perplexed. "He hasn't gotten away with this as long as he has by being sloppy. I mean, it's an awfully big risk to take when all he wanted was to scare me. It seems almost anticlimactic to imagine him making that kind of a mistake after being so careful for so long."

"Interesting." He strokes his stubble covered jaw. The narrow set of his eyes and the way his lips draw together tell me he doesn't agree. "I see it another way."

"By all means, enlighten me. I'm looking for answers."

"If this is him, and he took a risk like this, it wouldn't be a matter of sloppiness or carelessness. It would be his ego overriding the instincts that have gotten him this far. Do you think that's possible?"

Now that he put it that way, I see the other side of the coin. "That is normally how it happens," I muse, chewing my lip again while staring at the image. "The one mistake that breaks a case. When the perp is so full of their own cleverness, and so convinced they're smarter than everybody else, they slip up."

"Exactly." He nods firmly before pushing away from my desk, arms folded. "It's usually ego that takes them down in the end. They get away with something long enough, they start to feel untouchable."

No need to ask myself what my gut thinks this time. "I believe that about him."

"At this very minute, he could be sitting back with a beer, laughing to himself at the idea of you feeling like your world is getting smaller because he's out there somewhere, watching."

And then it hits me. "Oh, come on. Where is my brain?" I jump from the chair and grab my coat from where it hangs over the back. "I need to go. I'm late as it is."

"For what?"

"I'm supposed to be meeting up with Mitch and my dad."

"Dinner with Dad this time? That's something."

I nod, distracted by pretty much everything swirling through my head as I fumble with my coat buttons and shove the phone into my pocket. "Yeah, this conference Mitch was supposed to go to got pushed back a day due to scheduling issues with the venue, and there's a big game tonight. He knows Dad's a football fan and he figured it would be nicer for him to watch the game around other people. It's a lot to explain."

"There's no need to explain," he says, though the concern in his voice says otherwise. "Are you sure you'll be all right, though?"

"If I could survive dinner with my mother, I can survive anything."

"That's not what I mean. Just hold on a second," he urges when I'm on my way around him, headed for the door. "Do you feel safe going alone?"

I didn't think about it until this very moment. I haven't been able to think beyond the next minute since I found that note. "I'll be fine," I decide. I'm not sure who I'm trying to convince, though. That's the problem.

"I could send you with a security detail. I know I would rest much easier tonight if you had backup."

The concern in his voice eases some of the fear that had me in its grip. "There's no need for that," I insist, giving him a smile and a firm nod. "It's only a short drive to the trailer park. And I'll be with other people, so it's not as if there won't be anyone to keep me safe from the bogeyman."

His jaw tightens while a disapproving look hardens his expression. It can't be easy having him as a father – he's kind and protective, for sure, but he has seen far too much of the evil humans are capable of to ever loosen his hold. I'm sure those kids can't get away with anything. "You sound pretty confident for someone I found sitting here staring blankly at the wall a few minutes ago."

He's not wrong. "You helped me put everything into perspective. If he's following me, he's playing a game. He's not going to come out in the open now, and maybe not ever. But if he does," I add, "I know how to take care of myself."

He holds up his hands in surrender. "Whatever you say, Agent Forrest. Enjoy the night."

I might have been able to enjoy it if it weren't for the ever present sensation of having eyes on me the second I'm outside. All I can do is move through life normally, because if there's one thing I know, it's that I'm not about to let this maniac dictate my choices now or ever.

21

ALEXIS

At least the rain stopped. That's about the only positive thought I can muster up on my way out of town, the car pointed in the direction of the trailer park. I'm already so late — a call to Mitch only sends me to his voicemail. "Hey," I call out since the phone is on speaker, "I'm on my way now. I'm so sorry I'm running late. Just another day at the office."

There's an almost manic sound to my voice, I realize, so it's better to end the message now than to say anything that might set off Mitch's Spidey senses. He is way too good at deciphering my moods.

And the last thing either of us needs is for him to find out about the little gift I discovered earlier. It would only ruin the night, and it's important to Mitch that he spend a little time with Dad and let him know there isn't any weirdness on his side of things. There's at least one person in town who won't judge him or shun him. I'm sure there are more, naturally, but Dad probably feels differently. I imagine he still feels the stares and hears the snickers during his infrequent trips to town. It's easy for me to say things aren't so bad when I'm not the one who has to face it.

I have no doubt things will go brilliantly. They won't if I spill the beans, though.

But every minute that passes puts me one minute farther away from the time a psycho placed a note on my car. A note he wrote on the back of a receipt he was handed hours ago. What am I doing?

My tires squeal as I pull a sudden U-turn, and I grimace at the sound of a blaring horn letting me know the driver approaching in the other direction didn't appreciate my sudden change of route. I ignore it and press my foot against the gas pedal, taking a direct route to the store.

I'm already late. A few extra minutes isn't going to hurt anything. It would be a far worse decision to go straight to my father's, then sit around and wonder what I might be missing by not hunting this man down.

There are three cars in the lot when I pull in close to the door. I'm overly cautious now, looking over my shoulder, checking the area around the building. He has to know I would come back here. Is he leading me on a wild goose chase? Watching from the deep shadows, hidden behind the tree line?

That's what he wants me to think. I'm not going to cripple myself with doubts and questions. Instead I march into the store and go straight to the register, where a kid who can't be older than twenty looks bored as anything, playing on his phone as I approach.

"I need your help," I tell him, noting he almost recoils at my sudden announcement. "You had a customer in here earlier who bought a handful of things. I need to see any video footage you have of that customer, as soon as possible."

He blinks rapidly. "Huh? Why? Who are you?"

Frustration is rising in my chest and tightening my throat, leaving my skin hot and prickly. "I need to speak to your manager immediately." Because obviously, I will get nowhere with this kid.

"Yeah, hang on a sec." He touches a button on the side of a microphone mounted to the counter. "Joe? You're needed at the register."

I look toward the back of the store, where a door opens to allow a middle-aged man through. He looks annoyed, which doesn't bode well. I'm sure he doesn't feel like getting pulled into yet another piece of customer drama. "What can I do for you?" he asks with a weary sigh when he reaches the register to find me waiting.

"You had a customer in here a few hours ago. I have reason to believe he's part of an investigation currently being conducted in Broken Hill. I'm going to need access to your video surveillance footage from around four this afternoon."

He blurts out a laugh. "Sure. And I'm going to need access to a hundred million bucks by morning."

With a sigh, I open my coat and hold up the badge hanging from my neck by a lanyard. "Alexis Forrest, FBI. Now please, show me where I can find the footage."

His expression softens, but it's clear he is still feeling put out. "It's in my office. You know exactly when this person was in here?"

I pull out my phone and check the photo. "Yes, I have a receipt here. Five minutes to four."

"Simple enough." He waves me along with him, then throws me a look over his shoulder as we walk to the back of the store. "Sorry if I came off harsh. You wouldn't believe some of the things I get called out here for. Everything from expired coupons to people trying to return items in open packaging with half the contents missing."

"No doubt." He opens the door to his office and ushers me inside. It's pretty bleak and cheerless, but then I didn't expect much else. A mug on the desk reads *World's Best Dad*. That's the only personal touch visible when I glance around the room before joining Joe at a laptop where he pulls up the feed from a handful of cameras.

"There isn't an inch of space that goes uncovered, is there?" I observe as he searches for the time indicated on the receipt.

"Can't afford it," he murmurs without looking my way. "Company wants to be sure their assets are being properly monitored. Here we go. I dialed it back to 3:50, so you should be able to see the guy if he had to wait in line or something like that."

"Thank you. That's very helpful." We watch together, and I withdraw my notepad, prepared to jot down a description. I still remember the man I met at Hawthorne Academy – the same man whose photo we found in the cabin, holding up a fish. The image is burned into my brain.

But he could have changed his appearance. If he's smart, he would've grown a beard or a mustache, dyed his hair, he could even be wearing a wig. I can't pigeonhole myself by relying too much on what I've already seen.

A man in a puffy coat enters the frame at 3:54. He stands behind a young woman holding the hand of a kid who looks to be about five years old. He's carrying a basket with a few items inside. The hair rises on the back of my neck, and everything around me goes hazy as I zero in on him. *Look up. Look up. Look at the camera.*

"That him?" Joe asks.

"Don't know," I whisper, barely hearing him, barely aware of anything but what's happening in front of me. The woman and the little girl walk away, and he steps up to unload his basket on the counter. There's a sketchpad, markers, a bottle of Sprite. Almost as an afterthought, he grabs a bag of Sour Patch Kids from the rack in front of the register, then a bag of Skittles. His hair is a flat, mousy brown, cut short and receding a few inches from his forehead. He looks to be somewhere in his mid-fifties, which is roughly the age of the person we're looking for based on how long he's been operating.

He finishes paying with a card, then takes his bag before turning away from the register. I'm holding my pen tight enough to make my fingers ache, willing him to look up with all my might.

And then he does, and my breath catches. "Pause it!" Joe does as I ask, and I stare at the face in front of me. He was wearing a ball cap when we met, and the shadow concealed most of his face. But this could be him. This could easily be him. An icy finger traces its way down my spine and I shiver.

"What about cameras outside?" I ask once I snap out of my moment of mute recognition. He changes the feed until we're looking at the parking lot. The man in the puffy coat who may or may not be a serial killer gets into a Volvo with a clearly visible license plate whose number I jot down.

"Let me ask you. Is there any way I can get a hold of the information for the card he paid with? We need to track him down as quickly as possible."

"What did this guy do?"

"I'm not at liberty to discuss." And he is wasting my time. Every minute that passes could be a minute this man is getting further away. What if he already has someone with him? What if that's who the candy is for? The implications are enough to make my head spin.

He closes out the video feed and pulls up software I don't recognize. He types a few things, scrolls through a list of entries, then clicks one of them and pulls up the credit card number, along with the name attached to it. "Thank you so much," I tell him after taking everything down with a trembling hand. This is it. This could really be it.

But I'm also running late, and I have people waiting for me. While I want more than anything to go back to the station and dig into this, I call the captain, instead. Rather than try to reach his office I call his cell, assuming he's left for the evening.

"Alexis? Are you all right?" The concern in his voice leaves me smiling a bit regretfully. I don't like thinking about him being worried, even if it's on my behalf.

"I'm fine. I made a pit stop at the CVS."

He groans loudly. "I should have known you'd go there rather than go straight to dinner."

My tingling skin and racing heart don't react to his disapproval. "I saw him on the camera. I have a description and a license plate for his car and the number to the credit card he used when he paid."

"Good work. Let's have it. I can run this down while you're having dinner."

I rattle off the information before adding, "It could be him. I saw his face. I wish I had gotten a better look at him the day I spoke with him." How could I know?

"We'll have a better idea once we find out who the car is registered to. It shouldn't take long — I'll get back to you as soon as I have anything."

And I have to trust this can be managed without my having a hand in it. I've already done as much as I can. All that's left now is compartmentalizing, to push all of this aside and put on a happy face for the sake of people who deserve more from me than worrying about yet another case.

Even if it might be the biggest case of my life.

22

ALEXIS

And there I was, thinking they would miss my company now that I'm showing up so late. It seems nothing could be further from the truth as I'm ushered into Dad's trailer, where Mitch is already sitting on the sofa with a half dozen alcohol-free beer cans scattered around. He was even thoughtful enough to bring alcohol-free beer for my father. When I think he's done all he can to steal my heart, he decides to surprise me.

"I was starting to worry about you." To my surprise, Dad is distracted and hurried as he helps me out of my coat, then hangs it near the door before returning to the game. Maybe I shouldn't be surprised. He's always been a devoted football fan, and some things never change.

"I left Mitch a voicemail, letting him know I was running late." I lift an eyebrow in my boyfriend's direction.

He counters with his own raised eyebrow. "Yes, ages ago. What took you so long? Is everything all right?" There's no harsh judgment in Mitch's questions. There's only concern as he rises from the sofa and comes over to give me a chaste peck on the cheek. He and Dad might be newfound best friends, but there are still lines he's not ready to cross, I guess.

"Everything's fine. I got caught up as usual."

Does he buy it? He seems to, since he begins helping Dad in pulling covered aluminum pans from the oven. "We kept everything warm for when you got here."

"I'm even more sorry I kept you waiting so long, then. I figured you would help yourselves."

"Nonsense," Dad insists, one eye on the TV as he pulls out plates and cutlery. "We weren't about to get started without you. I picked up lasagna from Chez Roberto."

The mention of what used to be our family's favorite Friday night dinner spot lodges a lump in my throat. It was where we always requested to go for our birthday dinners, too, and all other special occasions.

"I haven't thought about that place in a long time," I admit. "Are they still as good as ever?"

"To be honest, I haven't dined there in a long time, either." He wears a wistful grin as he lifts the lid from a steaming pan of aromatic lasagna. Just the sight of it is almost enough to bring tears to my eyes as memories come flooding back. I help myself to a large slab which I take to the coffee table and Mitch brings over a plate of garlic bread for us to share. I raise my eyebrows when Dad's back is turned, and he gives me a thumbs up, grinning. I'm not surprised. Not only could Mitch get along with just about anybody, but Dad is the same way. At least, he always used to be.

"How was your day?" Dad asks on returning to his chair, but before I have the chance to answer, he groans. "Holding? In what universe was that holding?" he demands, gesturing frantically toward the screen.

"That ref needs glasses or something," Mitch agrees, and soon the two of them are busy talking about the call. I don't mind; if anything, I love seeing them getting along so well. I'm glad they have something in common besides me.

I cut into my lasagna with my fork and spear a few layers which I carefully guide to my mouth. It's amazing how evocative smell and taste are. I close my eyes and right away I'm a kid again, sitting with my family at our favorite restaurant. Dad is telling his corny jokes to make Maddie and me roll our eyes, which we did with gusto. Mom swats at him with her napkin, giggling helplessly, which of course only ever added fuel to the fire. He loved nothing more than to make his girls laugh – something I heard him say more times than I can count. He always wanted us to be happy, and he loved knowing he was the one to provide that happiness.

If only I could make him happy now. Well, he seems happy enough in the moment, even if he's not thrilled with the ref who made that last call. On replay, I see why he's irritated, but my attention quickly shifts away from the game and back to the enormity of what took place today.

How long will it be before I hear something on our suspect? Is it him? Is this the man who placed our lives on the path we currently tread? If it weren't for him, would I still have a whole, complete family? Would my sister be off somewhere living the life she once dreamt of?

"What do you think?"

Dad's question stirs me from my reverie, and I find him watching me. "The lasagna," he prompts. "Does it hold up?"

"It does," I decide after taking another bite. "It's fantastic."

"There's something to be said for continuity," Mitch decides as he digs in during a commercial break. "You need things you can count on."

"Such as being able to get the greatest cup of coffee in the world at your shop?" I suggest with a wink.

"Yes," he agrees, because why waste time with false modesty. "Yes, I would like to earn that status. To be the place people return to because they know they're going to get good quality."

"That's one thing I sort of miss in a way." Dad's voice takes on a soft, thoughtful tone. "Being a regular someplace. Going back again and again, knowing they'll have my order cued up before I need to place it. It's a good feeling."

"You should come by the store," Mitch offers. "I'd love to see you down there."

I find myself holding my breath, waiting for Dad's reaction. Mitch understands it's a touchy subject, of course. We've discussed the way Dad has sort of made himself a recluse out here. Yet rather than bully him or nag him into coming out and being part of the world again, he takes a gentle approach the way he always does.

Dad chuckles and offers a warm smile I recognize easily. He's about to turn Mitch down. "Nobody would want to see me around."

"Says who?" Mitch counters with a grin. "I, for one, would like to be able to talk football with somebody who actually knows what they're talking about. There are so many bandwagon fans around here, it's ridiculous."

"I knew that would happen," Dad tells him with a laugh. "All dynasties must end their run eventually, and New England had two solid decades. It's somebody else's turn now."

"Why not Philly?" I ask, which leaves him raising his can in my direction.

By the time the commercials are over and the game is back on, my father lifts a shoulder. "We'll see. Maybe I'll stop in sometime soon to drink up the salty tears of disappointment." The three of us laugh before the guys turn their attention back to the on-field action.

Talk about a minor miracle. If Mitch can convince Dad to come back to life, what can't he do? Once again, for the hundredth time, I silently thank whoever was responsible for bringing him back into my life.

Their engagement with the game allows me to sink back into my concerns, knowing Dad is safely and happily occupied. I can let the commentary fade into the background of my awareness while wondering what I'm supposed to do next. I have to stop myself from twisting around so I can look out the window at our backs, wondering if there's someone watching. He wouldn't follow me out here, would he? Not after making contact today. He would stay away, protect himself.

But then why would he make such a monumental mistake and potentially lead me straight to him? If he were deliberately baiting me, planning on being caught, he wouldn't be the first. There have been cases throughout history where a killer was so sure of their cleverness and importance, the time came when they couldn't wait any longer to brag to investigators all about how they had evaded capture for so long. If this man has been killing for three decades, that time may very well have come.

But I don't buy it. My gut is telling me something is off. He's leading me on a wild goose chase — and he'll be watching as I eagerly take the bait. The idea sets my teeth on edge and makes fresh resentment bloom in my chest, leaving me no choice but to dig my nails into my palm while I continue eating like nothing is wrong. He touched my car. He has come so close to me.

I don't have much of an appetite now, but I force my way through a few more tiny bites before standing. "Anybody need anything?" I ask, picking up the empty cans and tidying up in hopes no one will notice how little I've managed to eat. It's a shame, too. The lasagna really is delicious.

"You don't have to do that," Dad insists. "You're my guest."

"Would you just let me take care of you, for heaven's sake?"

"It's better to stay out of her way when she takes that attitude," Mitch warns him.

"Oh, so you figured that out already?" Dad counters.

"Remember, I have past experience, too."

"That's right. I almost forgot about that." Dad's voice takes on a wistful tone. "I wish I could've been around then."

"You're here now," I remind him, kissing the top of his head as I pass. "That's what matters." And the man who ruined your life might have left a note on my car today. It would be the ultimate act of cruelty if I told him about that. He would never stop worrying, and neither would Mitch. I can't do that to them. Not even if I know for sure they would give me all kinds of attitude if they found out I was hiding something.

Besides, I would rather have concrete answers to offer, and right now, I have nothing. I won't know if the man at the drugstore is the man I've been hunting until we get more information from the plates and his credit card.

All I can do is sit back with the two men in my life and try to follow the game while watching the clock, hoping against hope to have answers before the night is over.

23

ALEXIS

"And you're telling me you made these yourself?" Dad sinks his teeth into his third of the chocolate chip cookies Mitch brought along for dessert. "You can't be serious. These are the best chocolate chip cookies I've ever had in my life."

"That's very kind of you to say." Mitch takes one for himself, then takes a bite before raising his brows. "You might be right. These might be the best chocolate chip cookies ever baked."

"Wow. Feeling pretty sure of ourselves, aren't we?" When I take a bite of the semi-sweet cookie with its flaky bits of sea salt, it takes real effort to not let my eyes roll back in my head. Dad doesn't need to see that, but he does get to hear me groan softly. There is only so much propriety a girl can practice when it comes to something this delicious.

"You could make a mint off of cookies," I tell him, reaching for a second though I'm not finished with my first.

"I hate to disappoint either of you," Mitch admits, "but this is the recipe from the back of the bag of chips. I add a little extra salt and extra vanilla, but that's it. I wouldn't feel right making a fortune off of a recipe I didn't develop."

"You could develop your own," I suggest. "I bet you could come up with something spectacular."

"If you need a taste tester," Dad adds between bites, "I would gladly volunteer my services. I can put a résumé together if you want."

The idea leaves me laughing. "What kind of experience do you have?" I ask, narrowing my eyes and tipping my head back to look at him over the bridge of my nose. "It's a competitive job market."

"I've eaten more than my fair share of cookies in my time."

"I'll let you know," Mitch tells him, grinning. "It would give you a reason to stop by the bookstore, too." He's not about to let it go. I sense Dad's mild discomfort around the topic being brought up again, but he manages to maintain his cheerful demeanor as he nods.

The buzzing from my phone, tucked in my back pocket, sends what feels like an electric shock through my body. Not the phone itself, but rather what the message might involve. I pull it out, holding my breath.

"Is everything okay?" Dad asks while I open the message from Captain Felch.

We have a name and an address. Heading over shortly.

My mouth has gone dry all of a sudden, and what's left of the cookie I was chewing now tastes like sawdust. "Is something wrong?" Mitch's voice is warm with concern.

"Nope. Everything's fine." Then why is it difficult for me to meet his gaze? "But I am sorry, I have to run. Something came up today, and I just got a text about it from Captain Felch."

Mitch is wary, studying my face like he's looking for the truth. Why am I so hesitant to reveal it? Mainly because I know how badly it would shake him up if he found out about that note. I'll tell him about it once this is settled.

I kiss both their cheeks, then whisper in Mitch's ear as I'm pulling on my coat. "I'm sorry. Are you going to be okay?"

"Sure," he whispers back. The game is about wrapped up, anyway, with only a few minutes left in the fourth quarter. "Call me later?"

"I will." Though I can't guarantee it will be tonight, depending on what happens. He'll understand once I give him the full story. He has to.

On my way to the car, I call the captain, my gaze sweeping the area before I check the back seat of the Corolla. Can't be too careful. "I need that address."

"This was not an invitation for you to join us."

The chiding tone in his voice leaves me gritting my teeth as I get behind the wheel of the car. "You can't expect me to sit back and wait for word of what you find at this guy's house when he could be the man I'm looking for."

His heavy sigh tells me he sees the point in this, but he doesn't like it. "I'll text it over. We're on the way now."

"Wait for me before you do anything, please." Then I end the call before he can give me an excuse why he won't honor my request, plugging the address into GPS before pulling away from the trailer. The house sits on the other side of town, in what I remember to be a decidedly lower middle-class area. Could he have been living there all this time? Or maybe it's a rental, someplace he found when he decided to return to his old stomping grounds.

All I know for certain is the car can't possibly move fast enough, and I'm glad for the practically nonexistent traffic on the road at this time of night. Most people are probably watching the end of the game, if they haven't already gone to bed.

A trio of patrol cars sit at the corner of the block where Sam Loften lives in one of a line of small, plain homes. I park behind one of them and Captain Felch meets me at my car. "We're going to surround the house," he tells me once I've stepped out, his eyes shifting back-and-forth, always watchful. "Once we have it secured, I'm going in with two of the officers. The lights are off, the house is quiet."

"I'm coming with you."

"Negative."

The flatness of his voice and the severity of his expression make my head snap back. "Because … ?"

"Because we don't know how this guy is going to react. It's one thing for us to go in there, but what happens if he sees you? If this is the guy you think it is, your presence could make apprehending him that much more challenging."

"I am not trying to make your job more difficult. You know that. But I'm not waiting here. I want to see where this man lives. I want to see if there's anything inside that might be a hint of what he's planning next. I know what to look for," I remind him when he blows out an exasperated sigh.

"You can go in once we have him."

I see his point, and it makes sense. I wish it didn't. I wish I had some logical means of opposing his position. All I can do is appeal to his awareness of my history with the case. "Please. You know what this means to me. And you can use all the backup you can get. If this is who I think it might be, he's not going down without a fight."

He clenches his jaw and mumbles something under his breath before shrugging. "All right. I know better than to think you'll stay behind unless I zip tie you and leave you in one of the patrol cars." I follow behind him as he issues a final reminder to the team that the man we are about to apprehend could be armed and is potentially very dangerous. I have to wonder if he's reminding them, or me. Not that I need to be reminded. I know very well what he's capable of – if this is, in fact, the man we've been searching for.

"You armed?" The captain asks as we approach the house. Rather than offer a verbal response, I withdraw the semi-automatic I took from my glove box before stepping out of the Corolla. I'm not taking any chances tonight. We continue, a handful of deputies fanning out in front of us, surrounding the single-story structure with its rather shabby siding and a small, sagging front porch.

My heart is ready to pound out of my chest by the time we step onto the porch. The captain's radio crackles. "In position," one of the men announces. We exchange a glance before I nod firmly, and he raises his fist to knock on the door.

"Police!" he barks. Gone is the friendly, affable man who's become something of a mentor. I wouldn't want to go up against this forceful, commanding version of him.

We listen hard, all of us going still, but there's no response. There is, however, the sound of a door inside opening and closing, followed by a heavy tread somewhere in there. The captain knocks again, harder this time. "Police! Open the door."

This could be it. I want to kick the door down and storm in, but somehow I manage to remain in place. The captain motions for all of us to take a step back before a pair of men step up with a battering ram between them. Within moments, the door bursts inward and we follow it, storming the house with our guns drawn.

There is a high-pitched, frantic shouting going on at the far end of the house. "Stop, stop! I'm unarmed! Why are you here?"

There's a frenzy of activity in response. "On the floor! On your knees, hands in the air!" Everything happens so quickly, voices overlapping, with the sound of Sam's cries rising over the orders being barked at him. He's shaking and weeping as the zip ties are secured around his wrists and he's hauled to his feet. There's a sense of grim satisfaction in watching him being led out of the house, while Captain Felch reads him his rights.

Meanwhile, I take a cursory look around, and immediately my gaze falls on a sketchpad open on the coffee table of a cramped but cozy living room. There's an open bag of Skittles next to it, a few pieces scattered on the surface of the table. This is the man from the video.

The question is, is he the man I'm looking for? I follow Felch out of the house, prepared to head to the station for questioning while officers search the house for evidence. Any plans to process the scene have flown out the window.

I want us to share a room. To look each other in the eye.

I want him to know his game playing is over.

24

ALEXIS

"**P**lease, I don't understand!" Those are the first words out of Sam Loften's mouth when I enter the interrogation room. "What did I do? What is this about? You must have the wrong person!"

I've heard that more times than I can count, so his assurances fall on deaf ears as I take a seat across from him. He's still in his pajamas as he was when he was pulled from the house, consisting of a faded sweatshirt and a pair of plaid flannel pants. His thinning hair is disheveled, like he was roused from sleep by the knock on the front door. How nice of him, being able to sleep soundly when he's caused so much devastation and sleepless nights for so many others.

If this is the man in question. If it was him who left that note.

"Please." Tears roll down his cheeks as they have been since he was left alone in here while we discussed a game plan. I've been watching him on the monitor, studying his reactions, and so far there's nothing to indicate he's anything more than an innocent man. I'd hardly expect him to stroll in and announce he's a murderer, though, so his whimpering only irritates me as I take a seat. I need to remember who I'm possibly dealing with. I cannot underestimate him.

"Mr. Loften." My voice catches a little, and I clear it before starting again. "Mr. Loften, you have no idea why you're here?"

"No!" he insists. "I don't get it. What did I do? I was sleeping, I was home all night, I've never done anything wrong! Please, somebody tell me something!"

"Take a breath." What I want more than anything is to throw myself across this table, take him by his shirt and haul him in close, demanding he tell me the truth. I need to take a deep breath of my own in order to calm that impulse before it overtakes me.

"That's easy for you to say." He leans in, his dark eyes shining with fresh tears. His somewhat pudgy face is flushed, and his chin quivers pitifully. "I'm a theater teacher. That's all. I've never done anything wrong. I don't even have any parking tickets or moving violations. Nothing. You've got the wrong guy."

"You don't know what you're here for, so how can you be sure of that?"

"Because I never did anything," he insists again in a voice loud enough to make my ears ring. "I teach theater! Ask anybody who knows me. I go to work, I come home, that's it. That's all. Whatever I'm here for, it's a mistake, I swear!"

"Where do you teach?"

The sudden question startles him. It's about as effective as a slap across the face breaking him out of his panicked haze. "Broken Hill High."

I don't remember seeing him around while I was investigating Camille Martin's disappearance, but then I didn't interview every single staff member, either. "How long have you taught there?"

He sniffles before lifting his arm to wipe his cheeks on his sleeve. "Just this year. I moved from Arizona back in August."

New in town. That's easy enough to confirm. "And you taught there before moving here?"

"For twenty years. No, twenty-five," he quickly amends. "This is a nightmare. I can't even think straight. Why am I here? What do you think I did?"

I ignore the question in favor of staring at him until he meets my gaze. What am I looking for? Recognition. I'm waiting for the mask to slip, for him to reveal himself. If this is an act, he can't keep it up forever. He's going to make a mistake. All I can do is catch him in it. That means keeping my eyes peeled for anything that seems off, outside this frenzied state.

All I see is a man fighting to understand, staring at me in growing horror. The acrid odor of his sweat is beginning to waft through the air – I note the darkening around his neck and under his arms when he lifts them. "Why won't you tell me?" he asks. "Please. Don't I deserve to know why I'm here? I was only sleeping in bed."

"I have a few questions for you." I look down at my notes, very aware of my breath. In, out, I take my time. Is this all a game? Is he seeing how far he can get, whether he can convince me with his act? Heat flares to life in my chest and leaves me biting my tongue rather than blurting out anything that might come back to haunt me. "Did you run any errands yesterday, Mr. Loften?"

"Errands?" The question comes out high-pitched, and is quickly followed by the disbelieving laugh. "What, do you think I stole something? That's why you pulled me out of my house in my pajamas?"

"Please answer the question."

He runs a hand over his head, picking up the sweat beading there. "Yeah, I went to the drugstore on my way home after work. So what?"

"And what did you purchase?"

"I don't understand. What does this have to do with why I'm here? I've been to that store a dozen times."

"Answer, please."

He releases a growl of frustration before shrugging. "I picked up a sketchpad. We're starting to plan for our spring production, and I was trying to sketch ideas for the set. I grabbed a couple of snacks and a soda. I think that's it."

That checks out. "What did you do then?"

"I told you, I went home. I stopped at the store on my way. When is any of this going to start making sense?" he asks, shaking. "I didn't do anything. I swear. Bring in one of those lie detector things, and you'll see."

"I'm sure we can handle it," I tell him in as quiet and restrained a voice as I can manage. Is he sincere? He appears to be. I've never seen a man this undone during questioning.

He looks down at his hands and whimpers before a tear drips from his cheek onto the table. "I don't understand. I haven't done anything. None of this makes sense, it's like I'm still asleep and this is a nightmare."

"What did you do with the receipt?"

His head snaps up, brows drawn together. "The receipt? From the store?"

"Yes. Do you have it?"

He sits back in the chair, his mouth moving wordlessly before he shakes his head. "No, I tossed it out."

"When did you do that?"

"Outside the store? I guess?" His chin starts quivering again. "I didn't steal anything, if that's what you're asking. You can check my credit card and everything. I paid for my stuff."

"I assure you, we'll take care of that." I have to think. There's too much going through my head – too many questions, doubts, memories. He is still just as shaken as he was when we picked him up. Maybe more so, now that he's spent time in the station under these glaring lights, probably imagining any number of horrific things that could come out of this.

It's like he's reading my mind. "I could lose my job over something like this," he whispers. "Even false charges cause scandal, you know? I can't have this. You need to tell me what you think I did, because I swear I can prove I didn't do it. I don't know how, but I'll find a way. Because I know I've done nothing wrong, and things like this don't happen to innocent people. Right?" He needs me to confirm this. He needs me to soothe him. I'm not in a particularly soothing mood.

"Where did you throw out the receipt?"

He looks at the ceiling, releasing a soft, humorless laugh. "Outside the store. There's a trashcan right by the door. I put it in there and I went to my car. Is that a crime? Please, tell me, because last time I checked, it wasn't."

Is he telling the truth? I stare at the wall over his shoulder, trying desperately to remember the angle of the security camera and how much of the area it picked up. Was there a view of the can? I don't remember. "What did you do this evening?" I ask. "And is there any way you can provide an alibi?"

"Alibi? I was alone. Working. Having a snack, watching the football game."

"Did you stop off anywhere between the store and your house?"

"No. Didn't you already ask me that?" His eyes widen. "I know what you're trying to do. You're trying to trick me and trip me up. Why is this happening to me?" With his elbow propped on the table, he covers his face with his hand, his shoulders heaving as he sobs as quietly as he can manage.

What am I looking at here? A skilled liar? A hardened killer?

Or an average, everyday schoolteacher who found himself in a living nightmare?

"Sir, I have one final question for you." I fold my arms on the table and lean in, watching him intently. "Have we ever met before?"

"What?" He lowers his hand to reveal red eyes still leaking tears. "No. I don't know you. Why would you think that? Don't you know whether or not we've met?"

"I think I do." With that I push my chair back, standing and gathering my notes before leaving the room without another word. I'm shaking uncontrollably from head to toe and fighting hard to hold myself together by the time I step out into the hall.

Right away, the door to Captain Felch's office opens. "What do you think?" he asks after watching every minute of the interview.

"What do I think?" What a loaded question. "I think he's never seen me before tonight."

"Here's more good news," he informs me with a sigh. "The team combed the house, top to bottom. It didn't take very long. He doesn't have much."

"According to him, he's only been here since the beginning of the school year, so that tracks."

"Everything we pulled backs up his story," he informs me, eyeing the door behind which the miserable Sam Loften waits. "He moved in August. There were papers waiting to be graded on the kitchen table. He doesn't have a record, and he was even telling the truth about his lack of tickets. He's completely clean."

And I've been chasing my tail. I drive my elbow into the wall and grunt out my frustration. "He set us up. He set the whole thing up, and now he's sitting back and laughing," I growl while my head pounds a little harder with every word out of my mouth. I can see him now, laughing to himself, proud of his cleverness. How easy it was to lead us down the wrong path. All it took was pulling a stranger's receipt from a trash can.

He's an opportunist, this man. He doesn't just sit back and wait for his victims to wander into his trap. He can lure patsies, too, and that's exactly what he's done by leading us to Sam Loften.

I am no closer to finding him than I was before.

25

ALEXIS

"Have you slept at all?"

My head snaps up at the captain's question, posed mere hours after we released Sam Loften when we found nothing we could use to connect him with the note left on my car. He is freshly showered and well groomed, which I realize is in stark contrast to my rather disheveled state.

Sleep was an impossibility last night. Lying in the dark, staring at the ceiling, listening to the wind in the trees outside my window. Every so often one of them would blow close to the window, tapping against the glass like bony fingers tapping my suddenly fragile sense of security. And all the while, I imagined the man we know as Andrew Flynn out there. Watching me. Tapping the window the way he tapped on the back of my mind to let me know he's watching. Making sure I know he's nearby. That there's nothing I can do about it.

I was too exhausted to do more than step in the shower and go through the motions of washing up this morning. The braid I wound in my wet hair still hangs damp against my back, and I didn't have it in me to bother with makeup. The circles under my eyes would take too much time to cover up, anyway. And I don't have time.

Because not only is there a serial killer possibly watching me, but there is still a missing woman out there somewhere. I lost focus yesterday, worrying about myself, even if I know the man poses a threat to much more than just me. For all we know, he might have identified his next victim. He may even have captured them, and we simply haven't heard about it yet. There's much more at stake than my life.

I deliberately sit up straighter and hold my eyes open wider like I'm trying to prove something to the man gazing at me with concern from the doorway to my office. "I tried," I offer with a shrug. "Does that count?"

With a sigh, he folds his arms and leans against the doorframe. "You realize it weighs on my conscience, don't you?"

"What does?"

"Watching you work yourself to death."

His choice of words makes me wince. "For what it's worth, I'm not trying to do any such thing. I had a rough night, that's all."

"Nobody would blame you if you went back home and tried to catch a few winks."

"Negative. It can't happen."

"And why not?"

Because I tried for six solid hours and it got me nowhere. "Because I already reached out to Meredith and asked her to come in to speak with me."

"Trying to find whether she's come up with something else she mysteriously forgot to tell you about?"

"Something like that. Now that she's had a little time to think things over, she might remember what she neglected to tell me the first time around." I gulp down what's left of the coffee I grabbed on the way in, then instantly want more. "For all we know, Connor might have reached out to her to solidify their story. He might want her to feed me lies to get me moving in the wrong direction."

"And she may have been responsible for the whole thing," he adds, though I hear the doubt in his voice. When I look at him, searching for a reason behind it, he shakes his head. "I don't think you have to be the person to conduct an interview. You look like you're ready to drop."

"Do you think Alyssa Lawrence cares if I'm ready to drop?" I leave out the obvious part that I can't bring myself to say out loud. If she is still alive.

"All right. I'm not going to stop you." Not that he has a choice, and we both know it. I suspect that's a large part of what's behind his stern expression. That and my sharp, snappy tone.

At some point, I'll have to apologize for sounding sharp with him. At the moment, however, what matters most is getting Meredith in here. I offered to send out a car to pick her up, but she insisted she'd come in on her own after I promised not to keep her too long. Depending on what she's going to tell me, of course, I may have to go back on that promise.

For now, though, I want to know more about her relationship with Connor. Who is telling the truth here? Was he on the verge of breaking up with her? Were they really looking for a place together? Did he have a motive to get his wife out of the way?

I step out of my office in hopes of pouring fresh coffee from the break room into my empty cup, but the sight of Meredith being led into one of the interrogation rooms gets me sidetracked. It isn't so much the fact that she's arrived so soon after my early morning call, but more her appearance that stops me in my tracks. This is not the woman I met at the office, the one who braved slippery conditions in a pair of stilettos and a jean skirt that must have left her half frozen. Today, she's wearing a bulky sweater over a pair of leggings and a cute pair of ankle boots. It's still a cute outfit, but it doesn't seem to fit her aesthetic.

Her dull, limp hair and the absence of makeup are what I find the most interesting. She didn't take the time to fix herself up, though she made it clear she was going straight to the office after our discussion. Maybe she doesn't feel like she has to dress up so much if Connor isn't going to be around. Or maybe she's mourning the end of her relationship with Dr. Lawrence.

Curiosity overwhelms me. Rather than keep her waiting, I make a beeline for the room and enter before she's had the chance to get settled in. "Thank you for coming in on such short notice," I offer as we both take a seat.

"Like I said, this can't take long. Bridget's not in today, so there's nobody to answer the phones when I'm not there." She runs a hand through her hair, and I notice chips in her nail polish. Is this all for show? To make sure I know she isn't thriving so I won't suspect her?

"I won't hold you up." So long as you're honest with me. I leave that part unspoken and do my best to stifle a yawn before continuing. "How are you?"

She snorts and rolls her eyes. "How do I look? This has been a tough week."

"I'm sorry to hear that."

She arches an eyebrow and looks me up and down, while her lips tighten into a firm line. "For both of us, by the looks of it."

I'm going to let that one go, mainly because I don't have the energy to banter. "We still have a missing woman out there somewhere. I'm still trying to find her."

Meredith's jaw ticks and her teeth sink into her lip before her eyes start away from mine. "Yeah. That is a problem, isn't it?"

"What does that mean?" I can't help but notice her change in body language and attitude. I might go so far as to call her resentful, and I latch onto that, watching her intently.

"What do you think?" she counters with a soft snicker. "She's still out there. Poor Alyssa." Sarcasm practically drips from every word. Does she realize how this makes her sound? Does she care?

"Your opinion has changed?" I ask as gently as I can. "You seemed concerned before."

She rolls her eyes, folding her arms defensively. "It's just that, you know, life has to go on."

"I'm sure the people who love Alyssa would like nothing more than for life to go on."

"I know. I know, I'm being selfish." She shakes her head, sighing. "It wasn't supposed to be this way."

"What way is that?" There I was, imagining I would be the one to lead our conversation, but she's doing the work for me.

"We were supposed to be finding a place together. We were supposed to be starting something new."

I nod slowly, absorbing this, reading between the lines. There's a difference between letting her lead the conversation and allowing her to deliberately steer me where she wants me to go. So far, she isn't going over-the-top. Everything she's said sounds natural. Authentic. "And it didn't turn out that way," I softly conclude. "That has to be frustrating."

"Frustrating?" she asks with a humorless laugh. "We were better off before Alyssa went missing."

"How so? What's changed?" It's taking everything I have in me to adopt this friendly, conversational tone. Like we're a couple of girlfriends, catching up over coffee, commiserating about the men in our lives.

"I know what you're doing." She meets my gaze, and there's clearly resentment brewing in her eyes. "You still think I did something to her. I didn't. I never saw her as a threat. He always made it sound like he was, you know, days away from breaking the news. He strung me along."

She pulls a tissue from her coat pocket and blows her nose before groaning. "It's the world's oldest story. It's not like I liked having an affair with a married man. I would never have gotten involved with him if I knew he was just going to stay with her, anyway."

"Did he break it off with you?"

Her body sags slightly, almost like she's defeated, before she nods. "He tried to. I mean, I guess he did. He said, especially now that Alyssa is gone, he realizes what a mistake he made."

Her brows draw together and her face flushes before she barks out another laugh. "Now. He tells me that now. After all this time and everything we've been through."

It's more dramatic than reality TV. I give her a moment to compose herself before asking, "And this is the first time he ever tried to break it off?"

She heaves a sigh before shaking her head. "He felt guilty before. This isn't the first time. But he always came back around. I don't think he's going to do that this time. I think it's really over."

I'm not about to extend sympathy — yes, I feel sorry if she was duped, but there is a certain point where a person knows what they're getting into beforehand. It wouldn't feel right to console her, especially when the wife in question is still missing. "I'm sorry you were misled," I tell her, and I mean it sincerely. She's young. She may even have fallen in love. We don't always make the best decisions when in that sort of situation.

She checks her watch and groans. "I really have to go. Dr. Chetty is going crazy, handling everything by himself. He'll need me at the desk."

"Sure. Go ahead. Thank you for coming in." In the end, I've heard and seen enough. This girl is a mess, a far cry from the polished, sophisticated young woman I first met. This is a girl whose hopes have been dashed. She felt secure in her relationship with Connor until Alyssa went missing, telling me she didn't feel there was any reason to get her rival out of the way.

Of course, this brings me no closer to finding the person responsible. What am I missing? It could be I have to go back to the beginning and start over, but at the moment, I can hardly see straight for the exhaustion I can't seem to shake. This isn't the first time I've ever dealt with a sleepless night, though. I'm sure it won't be the last, either.

There's an excited cry from somewhere on the floor as I return from walking Meredith to the front door. "911 dispatcher just got a call," one of the deputies announces to the room at large. "There's a woman at the gas station out on Route 1 where it connects to the interstate. She said she's Alyssa Lawrence."

26

ALEXIS

I t is an absolutely frigid, unforgiving sort of morning, but I don't take time to wait for the heater to kick in before I peel out of the lot, prepared to fly down route one. Our officers could easily pick her up and take her to the hospital, but I have to see her for myself. I have to speak to her. I need to know this is the woman I'm looking for.

It isn't until I pass Mitch's shop on my way down Main Street that I remember I was supposed to call him last night. Well, I was unsure even at the time that I would get the chance, but it's morning, and I still haven't so much as sent him a text message. I should do that. Just because he doesn't get on my case for being forgetful doesn't mean he should go without hearing from me.

A spark of inspiration leaves me calling him while I'm waiting at a red light wishing I had a dome light and siren so I could get to the gas station faster. I doubt Mitch will be able to answer the phone at this time of day, when the store will be busy with customers grabbing a last minute latte before heading into work. I can at least leave him a voicemail to let him know I was thinking of him.

To my surprise, he answers the phone. "You had me worried," he says, foregoing a warm greeting.

I hear the message behind his statement, and guilt leaves me wincing. "I'm sorry. By the time I got home, it was so late."

"You could have texted."

It's rare for him to push this hard on an issue, telling me he is seriously affected by it. My heart sinks, and I murmur, "I'm sorry. Really. I know I need to be better at not letting myself get overwhelmed."

"What was it all about, anyway? What happened yesterday? You were distracted all night – it was obvious there was something on your mind that you didn't want to share. And I didn't want to press the issue, when I figured you were trying to keep your dad from hearing any details. Is it about the killer?"

I want to tell him. I do. I want it so much, I could cry. It's one thing for the captain to know about this – I don't have to keep it completely bottled up inside me. But there's something to be said for being able to rest my head on someone's shoulder and pour my

heart out. I want nothing more than that. To let
Mitch carry the burden for a minute or two while I
rest.

That would be unfair, though, and I can't do that to
him. He would only spend the whole day worrying.
Rather than tell him about the note, I settle for
vague details. "We thought we had him yesterday.
Last night, when I left all of a sudden. We thought
we found him living along the edge of town, on the
other end from the trailer park. But it wasn't him.
He is probably laughing at us as I speak."

"I'm sorry. No wonder you were in such a hurry to
get out. You could have said something, though. We
would have understood."

"You know I couldn't mention it in front of Dad."

"Right," he agrees with a sigh. "And I guess it's a
good thing you didn't, since it was the wrong person
in the end. No sense in getting his hopes up."

"Exactly." I'm getting closer to the station, and my
excitement grows with every breath I take.
"Meanwhile, a woman who says she's Alyssa
Lawrence is at a gas station at the turnpike on-ramp.
I'm headed there now."

"No kidding. There's never a dull moment, is there?"
Then, as if on cue, I hear a pair of voices in the
background. "I'd better go. The register's jammed.
Keep me posted, okay?" He ends the call before I

can promise to do so. I need to find a way to make it up to him, but right now, what matters more is getting to the gas station in one piece. I wish I'd had time to stop for some more coffee, though at the moment it would serve more as a means of warming me up than waking me up. Adrenaline has me wide-eyed and alert.

Is it her? And if so, what happened to her?

Dazzling sunlight gleams off the hoods of a handful of vehicles now gathered at the station. There are two patrol cars plus an ambulance, and as I pull in, a pair of paramedics take equipment from inside. A handful of bystanders and officers are gathered around what from a distance appears to be a gray lump.

Once I'm out of the car and jogging their way, I realize it's a woman sitting on a curb with a gray blanket wrapped around her. Her head hangs low, and dark, greasy hair hangs in clumps around her face. As I draw closer, she lifts her head slightly, and now I see the bruises covering her face. One of her eyes is swollen almost completely shut. She's trembling, and when someone asks if she knows what day it is, she only shakes her head while wearing a dazed expression.

One of the officers spots me lingering near the edge of the crowd. "All right, everybody. Unless you wear a badge or you're a paramedic, you need to clear some space here." He shoos everyone away before joining me. "She says she's not sure what happened to her. She's in shock. But she claims she's Alyssa Lawrence."

"She looks like her," I murmur. She's thinner, like she hasn't eaten in days, but she bears a strong resemblance to the woman I saw in the footage taken from the camera outside the Lawrence home.

"Alyssa?" I turn at the sharp, almost hysterical cry to find Connor Lawrence running from his SUV, still dressed in pajamas and a coat he didn't bother to button. He also didn't bother closing his door after bursting from his vehicle. His jaw is covered in thick stubble, and he looks like he's gotten about as much sleep as I have recently, but there's joy radiating from his face. Hope.

The paramedics step aside, and Alyssa looks up. Her mouth falls open and her arms shoot out. "Connor?" she sobs. He falls to his knees in front of her, gathering her up in a tight hug before the two of them weep in each other's arms.

27

ALEXIS

"We need to get her to the hospital." The paramedic finishes taking her blood pressure before standing, joining me a few feet away from where Alyssa still clings to Connor. She seems to have calmed down some since he first arrived, and now he takes off his coat and drapes it over her shoulders. I don't think I've ever seen a man look so relieved, so overjoyed. His hands are shaking and he can't stop blurting out what sounds like disbelieving laughter. As if he can't believe his luck.

I need to speak to her. I need her immediate impressions, before she gets to the hospital and is pumped full of whatever they need to give her to combat what I imagine is dehydration and exposure. If she only escaped hours ago, it behooves me to get as much information as I can, as quickly as I can.

I'm torn between duty and sympathy, going back-and-forth before finally crouching beside the happy couple.

"Are the kids okay?" I've heard her ask Connor that question at least three times. I don't know whether she can't remember the answer or if shock won't allow her to absorb the information.

"Just fine. Missing you, but they're fine." Connor meets my gaze and I offer a smile which he is slow to return. I don't doubt he's feeling conflicted toward me now, since I pulled no punches when it came to questioning him.

"Mrs. Lawrence. I'm so happy to see you. My name is Alexis Forrest," I offer in a soft but firm voice. I'm careful to give her space rather than crowd her after whatever it is she's been through. "I know you must be exhausted and you want to see your kids, but it's my job to find whoever did this to you. If there's anything you can share with me now that I can relay to the officers in town, it would be tremendously helpful. We want to find these people and punish them."

"Hasn't she been through enough?" Connor asks, and the grip he has on her tightens when he pulls her close.

"I understand your feelings," I tell him as gently as I can, "but I would also imagine you want justice now.

I know I would. The sooner we track these people down, the better for everyone involved."

"She's only trying to do her job," Alyssa whispers to him, and some of the concern melts from his tightened features. "I understand. I'm just so fuzzy. I don't know how much I can remember."

"I completely understand." I back off a little when one of the employees at the gas station brings her a cup with steam rising through the hole in the lid.

"Some tea for you," the woman offers. "You must be freezing."

"Thank you so much." Alyssa offers a shaky smile as she accepts the beverage, holding it tight in her trembling hands. "That's nice. I'm so cold."

"Alyssa, is there anything you can tell me right now that I can use to put out an all-points bulletin? A car description, a description of whoever held you? Even the littlest details could help."

She takes a few sips of the tea and sighs, her eyes closing. Taking a deep breath, she says, "It all happened so fast. I was so scared. I thought I would never see my family again."

"You're safe now." Connor rubs her back as tears fill his eyes. "You're safe. No one is going to hurt you."

She nods as a tear that hangs from her bottom lashes spills over and runs down her cheek. "I was running," she whispers. "I was thinking about the kids. It sounds selfish now, and I beat myself up the whole time after, but I was actually thinking how nice it was to have a little time to myself. Without them. It's awful, it's a terrible thing, and I was punished for it."

"Don't say that," Connor whispers.

She shakes her head before continuing. "I remember it was kind of gray and wet, but it wasn't a bad day. All of a sudden, this van pulled up next to me and somebody jumped out."

"Can you describe the van?" I ask, taking notes with a hand that trembles either from the cold or anxiety.

"I don't know. It was white. No windows in the back. That's really all I saw. All of a sudden, the person who jumped out shoved me inside. I didn't even have time to react – and when I tried to scream, they put a gun in my face."

Her trembling intensifies, and a pained expression pinches her features. "You know, you can tell yourself all you want how you would react in a situation like that, but when there's a gun in your face, everything you thought you would do goes away."

"That is perfectly normal," I murmur. "It's easy to think you'll fight back until the moment comes."

"Exactly. That's exactly right." Her eyes shine like she's grateful for my understanding. "Anyway, they told me to be quiet or they would kill me."

"Can you describe them?"

She shakes her head. "They always wore black ski masks and black clothes."

"Masks? So this was more than one person?"

Her head bobs up and down. "There were two of them. They were both women."

By now, even the paramedics are listening to every word, and a murmur of surprise rises up over the group. I can't help but be a little surprised, myself. It's rare to hear of a crime like this perpetrated by women, but it's not unheard of.

"I was so scared," she whispers. "The one who threw me into the van kept the gun pointing at me while the other one drove. I was afraid to breathe or move or do anything. All I could think of was the kids and my husband and how I would never see them again." Connor touches his forehead to hers, shaking like she does.

A van. Two women dressed in black. "Did you recognize their voices?"

She sniffles and shakes her head. "No. They were strangers."

"What happened next?" It seems like she's loosened up, like the story is flowing more freely, and I'm not about to lose this opportunity while her memories are still fresh. Connor looks resentful, his brows drawing together, but I ignore him for the time being.

"They drove to a garage. That's how it looked, but I couldn't see much through the windshield when I was in the back of the van. They left the van inside the garage and left me in the van. I never left it. There was a bucket for me to relieve myself, and they would bring me a little bit of food now and then, but that was it. Every time I saw them, they had their masks on. All I could do was sit there in the dark van and try to stay warm, but that was no use."

"Poor thing." Connor's voice shakes, and he gathers her in his arms again. "My poor, brave girl."

"We really do need to get her someplace warm where she can be treated," the paramedic reminds me. I nod, waving a hand to show I understand, but a sense of urgency drives me to ask more questions.

"Is there anything at all you can tell me about them? Was there anything special or unusual about their voices, about their body shape? Tall, short, thin, overweight?"

"They were both overweight," she's quick to tell me. "And they sounded older. Their voices, I mean. Like maybe they were in their late forties or early fifties? I don't know what makes me think that, but that's the impression I got."

"Did they have accents?"

"Oh, they were local. New England, for sure."

"They ever use names?"

She shakes her head, wearing a disappointed frown. "No. And they didn't spend much time in the garage, or in the van, either. But I listened hard every time they came around." She lifts a hand to brush tangled hair away from her face, then winces when she notices its condition. "I'm a mess. I can't believe this is happening."

"How did you get away?"

"I … " Her voice is softer now, rather distant. "I'm sorry, but I'm so tired. I'm so cold."

"That's it, no more questions," Connor decides. "She needs treatment. That's what matters more than anything."

While I understand where he's coming from, there's still the matter of finding the people responsible. Yet he's helping her to her feet along with the paramedics, gently ushering her to the ambulance. I'll follow them to the hospital, of course, where I hope Alyssa will be better inclined to share anything else she remembers once she's more comfortable.

Why would anyone kidnap her and hold her all this time without taking things further? Why leave her in a garage for days?

Once Connor has made sure Alyssa is secured in the ambulance, he turns toward his SUV. "I have to ask you something," I venture, trotting alongside him. "Did you receive any sort of communication from someone? A ransom demand, something like that?"

"Don't you think I would've told you if I had?" Now that Alyssa is safely away from him, he can allow his bitterness to leak through. "Honestly, Agent Forrest. I'm becoming more and more inclined to believe you're only good at chasing your tail." Anything else he has to say is cut off when he slams the door, then starts his engine. I have no choice but to step back, fighting off the frustration his words have stirred in me. There has to be something she's forgetting, something that will tie her kidnappers to her. Otherwise, based on the description she's provided, I can't imagine how we'll ever find them.

With that in mind, I race behind the ambulance, following Connor's SUV. I need to make sure her clothing is properly processed for any evidence that might have been left on it. Right now, it's all I have to go on.

28

ALEXIS

Once Alyssa's clothes are bagged, I hand them to one of the officers who met us at the hospital. "Go and get these to forensics," I tell him. "We need them processed for any fibers or hair that might've been left behind." Right now, that's all I can do while waiting for Alyssa's assessment by the doctor. For the sake of privacy, they took her directly to a room rather than forcing her to wait in the bustling emergency room. It seems she's still overwhelmed, jumpy, affected by bright lights, alarms and voices.

She's in a private room, one with windows running along the length of the wall between it and the hall so she can be observed by the medical staff without them needing to go in and disturb her when she's asleep. At the moment she is sitting up in bed, answering questions, occasionally running a trembling hand under her eyes to catch errant tears. The woman has been through so much, and the struggle isn't over yet. As much as I hate to overwhelm her in her fragile state, we will need answers. Sooner rather than later, too.

The sense of letting her captors get away with it makes my skin feel too tight, itchy. There must be something I can do while waiting for her to regain her strength and get her thoughts in order. Once again, my hands are tied, and the truth of that leaves me grinding my teeth as I pace the hall in front of her room, waiting for a chance to go in and speak with her again. At least Connor headed home for a bit to pick up clothes and toiletries for his wife. I won't have him hanging over me, reminding me of how I suspected him. I hope he'll understand one day.

"Alexis."

At first, I'm sure I must be imagining things. I'm sleep deprived to the point where I'm hallucinating my boyfriend's approach. There's no hallucination about it. It really is Mitch marching down the hall, his pace quickening once he identifies me standing here, watching him.

I may be tired, but there's nothing wrong with my eyes. It becomes clearer the closer he gets that he is not happy. "What are you doing here?" I ask as I stand to meet him. "Are you all right? Did something happen?"

"Yeah, something did happen." For once, there's no twinkle in his eye as he stares at me. No music in his flat, tight voice.

"What is it?"

"Somebody came in earlier for a cup of coffee and asked if you were okay. Somebody who was concerned about you." When all I can do is blink in confusion, he groans. "Captain Felch."

So this is what betrayal feels like. This burning sensation in my gut. "Why did he do that?" I whisper, even though I very well know the answer.

"Because he said you looked half dead this morning, and he's not wrong. I had a feeling I'd find you here if you weren't at the station, and look. Here you are." He throws his hands into the air.

"I'm doing my job."

"Are you? Who assigned you to keep watch here?" he counters. "Your boss at the Bureau? Because last I checked, that's who you report to. You can't keep pushing yourself like this – and you can't keep pushing me away," he adds.

"How am I doing that?" I can hardly process everything he's throwing at me all at once. "I would never push you away."

"Really?" He folds his arms, scowling, and his baby blues seem to darken when they lock on mine. "So why didn't you tell me about the note you got?"

That settles it. I'm going to have a conversation with Felch over this. "He had no business—"

"I don't wanna hear it," Mitch insists, cutting me off. That's unusual for him, but then all of this is unusual. I've never seen him like this, even when we were kids. He's usually so even-tempered and easygoing. Until now, all I've ever received from him is gentle understanding. There's been concern mixed in there, sure, but there was never this angry edge to it. "He shouldn't have needed to tell me about it, because you should have been the one to do it."

"I was going to!" I whisper fiercely, keenly aware of the hospital staff passing in both directions. "Not yet."

"Why not? Why wait? Don't give me some nonsense about trying to protect me."

"What if that's the truth?"

His scowl deepens. "It's pitiful. I'm a grown man. I don't need you to shelter me from anything."

"Tell me. What would've been the point? If I ran to you and poured my heart out without knowing anything about the origins of that note, what would it have solved?"

"That's not the point, Alexis." He scrubs a hand over his hair, groaning, gritting his teeth like there's so much he wants to say but doesn't dare. "I want to be there for you. I want you to feel like you can share things with me. If you're scared, I want to know. If you're worried, overwhelmed, that's what I'm here for. All you can offer is secrecy disguised as concern for me, and I refuse to accept it."

The only term I can come up with to describe how I feel is shell shocked. The man in front of me now is miles away from the Mitch I've fallen for all over again. "I'm sorry," I whisper, feeling helpless. "That's all I can say right now. I couldn't tell you about it while we were at Dad's, of course. I didn't want him to freak out. You have to understand that, right?"

"That, I can understand," he admits. "But I was on the phone with you earlier. What's your excuse for that?"

"The fact that you were at work? Mitch, we could go back and forth about this all day. The fact is, I simply haven't had the chance to tell you about it yet. I was going to, I swear. I'm not trying to sneak around and hide things from you. But it's so complicated."

His weary sigh speaks volumes. I watch the anger drain from him, replaced by something that frightens me more. Sadness. Resignation. "The way I see it, it's not so complicated at all. You're so determined to keep everything to yourself while there's someone who wants more than anything for you to let him in. Until you can see that … I don't know what we're supposed to do. But I know I'm not going to pretend to be happy about it."

"I understand."

He quirks an eyebrow. "Do you? I'm not so sure."

"What are you trying to say?"

"Nothing. Don't listen to me." He shakes his head, still scowling. "I just don't know how we are supposed to make this work if I have to doubt whether you are telling me the full truth about your job and the danger you might be in. I think it's only fair to be angry and feel like you're keeping me at arm's length. That's not where I want to be."

"You have to know I would never do that on purpose to hurt you."

"But that's the thing. You don't have to do it on purpose to cause harm." With that, he turns on his heel, ignoring me when I call his name in hopes of making him stop so we can work this out. I guess it's for the best that he goes – no sense in fighting in public. I wish somebody would explain it to my heart, which sinks a little further with every step he takes until he disappears around the corner.

It's like I fell and got the wind knocked out of me. It's difficult to take a breath, to focus on anything but the sudden panic Mitch's appearance stirred up. What if this is it? What if he doesn't want me anymore? I was only trying to protect him, but I might have ruined the best thing that's happened to me as long as I can remember. I can't blame the captain, either, as much as I would like to. No, this one's on me. I know how Mitch feels about secrecy, no matter the motive behind it. I can only hope this is something we can grow from as a couple. That he'll give me the chance to make it up to him.

There couldn't come a better time for Alyssa's doctor to leave her room, since I need something to distract from the tightness in my chest. "How is she doing?" I ask once he joins me in the hall, leaving her by herself for the first time since she arrived at the gas station.

"As well as can be expected after everything she's been through. She'll need time and rest, but there's no reason she shouldn't make a full recovery. "

"That's good to hear. Did she share anything else? Any memories?"

He shakes his head, already backing down the hall. "Not yet, but once she's hydrated and has food in her, there's a chance she'll be able to think clearly again." There are plenty of other patients under this roof, and I guess he can't spend all of his time focused on a single individual.

But I can. I look away from the back of the retreating man and gaze toward the window to Alyssa's room.

Just in time to find her leaning back in the bed, resting her head against the pillows. She stares at the ceiling before a soft smile tips the corners of her mouth upward. Her chest rises and falls in what at first glance I can only describe as a satisfied, relieved sigh.

I've seen victims of kidnapping. More of them than I can count. Most recently, there was Camille Martin, who may have been younger than Alyssa but certainly went through her share of trauma. She was shaking, weak, and crying even after time spent safe and secure in her hospital bed. Even with her parents by her side.

She certainly didn't seem anywhere near as self-assured and steady as Alyssa Lawrence now does. The opposite of how she appeared only moments ago, in the doctor's presence.

I'm not sure what I'm looking at, but it's enough to raise the hair on the back of my neck.

29

ALEXIS

I have to be careful with this. Like walking through a minefield. If I take the wrong step, everything could blow up in my face. The beeps and alarms and chatter go on around me as I approach the door to Alyssa's room, yet they fade into the background, overshadowed by what looms ahead of me.

"Hi, there." I hover in the doorway with a cup of coffee in each hand. "They have a Starbucks in the cafeteria. Can you believe it?"

Her eyes light up at the sight of the cups. "Would you believe I craved Starbucks when I was gone?"

"I'm sure you did." I step into the room, leaving one of the cups on the wheeled table which she pulls across her lap before eagerly opening the lid and taking a sip. Something told me this would be a surefire way to earn a little trust.

"It tastes like normalcy." Her smile is wide and genuine, and I can believe she's grateful. But is she telling the truth? If it hadn't been for what I saw earlier, the way she changed when she thought no one was looking, I wouldn't doubt her. At least, not yet. It might take time to poke holes in her story.

Now, I find myself watching every facial twitch, every move she makes. Listening to her tone of voice and the words she uses. There's a slight twinge of guilt that goes along with this. Aren't we supposed to believe victims?

Yes, *if* they're victims. I need to find out for sure whether the woman before me qualifies.

"How are you feeling?" I ask, taking a seat in a chair close to the bed. Giving her space, making sure she doesn't feel crowded.

"Like I just woke up from a nightmare," she murmurs, then releases a soft chuckle. "And I'm still a little groggy, you know? Foggy headed."

Is that true, or is she already setting up a defense in case I ask a question she doesn't feel comfortable answering? Shock and memory issues can cover up for an entire range of sins.

"I can only imagine. You've been through an experience few people survive."

Her shoulders roll back and her chin lifts. That was the right thing to say. It bolsters her. "Even if I have this to remember it by. All these people want to interview me, and I look like this." She motions to the bruises on her face. "But I guess that's what makeup is for, too."

"Interviews?"

"News stations, that kind of thing. I don't know if I have it in me to talk about the experience yet." She rests her head against the pillow wedged behind it and sighs softly, wearily. "Though if it means helping one more person get through their own aftermath, maybe that's what I have to do."

Interesting. "It might be best to refrain from interviews until we've solidified a few points," I suggest. "There might be aspects of the case which shouldn't be discussed until we've tracked down the location where you were held. Wouldn't want to give your kidnappers the heads up that we're on their trail."

"Oh. I didn't think about it that way." She sounds crestfallen. "Sure. Whatever works. I definitely don't want them to get away with this."

"I didn't think you would." Sipping my latte, I ask, "How did you keep yourself from losing it?"

"I honestly don't know. I slept a lot. It was easier than being awake."

"I guess it was. You were so cold and everything. Probably hungry," I add.

"Starved – though, after a little while, that didn't bother me as much."

"Sure, you got used to it." Her head bobs before she takes another gulp. "They must've fed you something, right?"

"Every once in a while. When they remembered." She rolls her eyes. "I'd get toast, maybe a peanut butter and jelly sandwich. A sleeve of crackers. No actual food."

"Enough to keep you living."

"Pretty much." Her lips stir in a smile. "They're going to give me anything I want from the cafeteria. I never imagined looking forward to hospital food."

"It's pretty good here, from what I understand." I take another sip, biding my time. It won't look good if I bombard her with tons of questions. She won't be much use to me if she clams up. "And they left you alone otherwise? Didn't they have anybody guarding you?"

She lifts a shoulder, her teeth scraping her bottom lip while she plays with the cup. Avoiding my gaze. Not a great sign. "Every once in a while, I would overhear the women talking outside the van. They could have been out there for all I know, sitting next to me, but there were no windows for me to see through. All I could make out was the wall in front of the van through the windshield and the windows on the doors."

Her chin starts to quiver, her voice shaking. "Once, I woke up and there was a man looking at me through the front passenger window."

"A man? Can you describe him?"

She shakes her head. "I was so scared, and I didn't want to look at him. I was afraid if I made eye contact, he might, I don't know. Be angry. Like what if I wasn't supposed to identify him or something, you know? It's all a blur now."

"Did you ever see him again?"

"There were other men, but all they ever did was look at me. I ..." She takes a shaky breath and fans her hand in front of her face like she's fighting back tears. "Sorry. I don't want to get all emotional."

"No, it's okay," I assure her as gently as possible. "I'm sure it must be terribly difficult to talk about."

"I just have to keep reminding myself it's over now. In the past."

"That's right."

"Anyway," she continues, "they were talking about trafficking me."

Nothing about this story makes sense. Left in a van? It never occurred to her captors that she might be able to escape if they left her alone in the garage? They threw around the idea of trafficking her while hanging around the garage rather than having a conversation inside the house? "Exactly what words did they use? Can you remember? Did they use names, discuss where to send you or who would take you?"

She shakes her head. "All they kept talking about was money. How much they could get for me. I guess they were fighting about it or whatever, and they never made up their minds."

"Because they never did anything with you."

"Right." She laughs quietly. "I've never been so glad of anything, I think."

Nodding slowly, I grunt my agreement. "I guess you got out of there before they could go ahead with any plans."

"I guess I did."

"What was going through your mind?" I ask. "How did you manage to keep yourself together? I don't know what I would do in that sort of situation." I make sure to add a heavy dose of admiration to my voice in hopes of drawing her out, since she seems to respond well to the notion of being a heroine and sharing her story.

"You don't know until it happens to you," she tells me. "And honestly, I'm not sure. I did a lot of thinking about how I would try to escape."

"What were you thinking of doing?"

"That's the thing." She offers a shy chuckle "I never really came up with anything. It was more like, you know. I'll punch this one and kick that one and run screaming. It was more like a fantasy. But it was all I had to hold onto, you know?" Her voice trembles pitifully, and she wipes a tear from her cheek. "I don't mean to keep getting emotional like this. I'm sorry."

"You don't have to apologize," I murmur. "Really, nobody would expect you to have it all together after everything you've been through. You're allowed to feel the way you do."

"I don't want to sound like a victim. I think that's what bothers me the most. Like I was too weak to save myself."

"I don't think anybody considers you weak."

"Well, that's good to hear." Her smile is brief. "You never think something like this could happen to you."

"I'm sure. But you made it through. That's what's important."

She nods, her jaw tightening with determination. "That's what I keep trying to tell myself. I survived. I'm a survivor."

In all the times I've interviewed victims, I have never heard them talk about themselves this way so soon after escaping or being rescued. No, it's nothing I could use to prove she's lying—if she is, which I'm still not sure of. But to jump so quickly from a woman who could have been trafficked and was lucky to escape with her life to the brave survivor? I would think she would be more interested in identifying the people who held her captive, describing her surroundings if possible. That sort of thing.

And she has still not described how she escaped. I toy with the idea of asking her now, but it might be too much for her if everything she's told me is true and she is a genuine victim.

I can't believe I'm questioning whether she's telling the truth. How quickly things have changed.

"All I could think about was surviving and getting away," she explains. "It was what kept me focused. I couldn't just, you know, roll over and die. I needed to stay strong."

"So that was what took up most of your thoughts?"

Her head bobs up and down. "That, and worrying about what they might do to me next."

I wait, expecting more. When she takes her time, finishing her drink, I prompt, "And I guess you were thinking about the kids, too."

"Oh, sure." Her voice is a little louder, a little brighter. "Of course, they were on my mind the whole time. That goes without saying."

Does it? I have to wonder. Would she have mentioned the kids at all if I hadn't? She hasn't yet. Not even at the gas station.

"I've already taken up too much of your time." Some shred of self-awareness will not let me stay in this room with this woman another minute. I'm afraid if I do, I'll end up giving away my skepticism. Her story does not add up in the least.

It looks like the Alyssa Lawrence case isn't quite wrapped up yet.

30

ALEXIS

My head is spinning as I leave the hospital. The bracing air that smacks me in the face once I've stepped outside clears up some of the fog left over from my sleepless night, but not all of it. I have the feeling it's going to be a while before I manage to get any decent rest now that there's an entirely new layer of questions and doubts swirling in my mind.

Is she telling the truth? Am I completely off-base with my doubts? There's never any telling how an individual will react to a situation like this. I need to keep that in mind, but there's also the question of what she seems focused on. Not her husband or children, but sharing her story.

There's only one person I trust as a reliable sounding board, even if my irritation hasn't waned any. Felch had no right to stick his nose in where it didn't belong. He thought he was being helpful, I guess. Regardless of his motives, I have to put it aside for the sake of professionalism.

He sounds distracted when he answers my call, but there's something different in his voice from earlier this morning. He isn't so strained. What a shame I'm about to ruin that.

"How is our victim?" he asks.

"Resting comfortably. I'm leaving the hospital now after having a talk with her."

Though I haven't gone any further, I hear him sigh. "But?" he asks, his voice heavy.

"But … I don't know."

"What don't you know?"

"Whether or not she's telling the truth."

"Really?" He's exasperated, though at least he tries to stifle the worst of his reaction. "You're still uncertain?"

I'm a little more concerned with the fact that he isn't uncertain. I'd like to close this case as much as the next person, but only once we have the facts. "Something about her story doesn't add up for me. You're always asking me about what my gut is thinking, right?"

"Sometimes your gut is a bit too cynical," he grumbles.

In other words, my gut is telling him something he does not want to hear. After days of bearing the brunt of public pushback over the time it was taking to locate Alyssa, it's understandable he would want to put an end to all of this. He wants to consider it a win, and so do I, but not until I have the full story. I don't have it in me too celebrate a win I don't think we've earned yet.

"There's something not right about all of this," I insist on my way to the car, my shoulders hunched against the wind whipping through the concrete garage. "I don't know exactly what it is yet, but it's there. I feel it. I honestly think she's fabricating at least part of her story."

"Or she's in shock and still trying to piece everything together."

"That's completely possible, which is why I didn't give her any hint of doubt. I was nothing but sympathetic."

"So what are you saying? You think she ran off for a while? An overwhelmed young mother stages her own kidnapping, takes it easy, then wanders back into everyone's life?"

"She wouldn't be the first woman who ever needed a break," I point out. "Who knows? There doesn't have to be anything malicious behind this. Think about the IVF treatments, for instance. That's a lot of emotional strain to be under, finding out it was unsuccessful. That, on top of her unhappiness with Connor and all the trouble they were going through, not to mention the stress of keeping up the supermom image…"

He grunts, but I hear the hesitation behind it. "This is still a lot of trouble to go through if all she needed was a quick break."

I can only chuckle when I think about all the times I've wanted to take a break from life. Who hasn't? "I'm not going to disagree with you on that."

"What else has you doubting her?"

"Everything," I admit. "I know how it sounds, but there is simply something about her story that doesn't add up. She hasn't started to describe how she escaped, for one thing. She was supposedly held in a van in a garage all this time, yet she can't identify anything about the location or the people who held her there or any specifics at all. Now, I ask you, if you were a trafficker who happened to stumble across a woman you thought would make you money, would you hold her for all this time without doing anything with her? Or would you unload her quickly, get rid of her and make your money? It would've been risky, keeping her all this time."

"So they weren't experts. This might have been their first time."

I have to take a deep breath rather than blurt out something I can't take back. I might understand how desperate he is to wrap this case up, but he's trying a little too hard to explain things away. "It seems like a pretty risky endeavor if it was their first time."

"You saw the condition she was in. She was a mess. You mean to say you think she beat herself up? Starved herself to lose weight and make everything more believable?"

I might slam the car door a bit harder than necessary after sliding behind the wheel. "All I'm saying is, she might have made a rash decision. People do it all the time. Now, she has to come up with a believable excuse. I'm not making any judgments. I only want to find the truth."

"And how do you envision that happening?"

"I don't know yet." Wiggling my fingers in front of the vents, I sigh happily once they warm up. When you're beyond the point of exhaustion and your boyfriend is mad at you, it's the little things that make a difference. "I think our first step is to make sure the forensic lab carefully checks her clothing for DNA evidence."

"It's being done as we speak." He sounds a little perturbed, but all things considered, I'll let it go. He might have been on top of the world, beyond relieved before I called and shook things up.

"For what it's worth, I don't want to not believe her. I want this to be a happy ending, but I can't ignore the red flags."

He sighs again, but the sound isn't quite as heavy this time. "No, you don't have to explain that to me. I'll keep you posted on anything we hear from the lab."

It's probably a good idea to end the call here, so I do, only releasing a frustrated groan once I know he won't be able to hear. It's just me and my otherwise empty car, still sitting in the hospital parking garage.

Mitch would understand if Mitch was still talking to me. He knows I've always been able to tell when a person is lying, even when I want to believe them. My heart aches at the thought of him and how angry he was – and still is, I'm sure. I doubt things have blown over already. I don't want us to fight.

It looks like I have to be the bigger person and reach out first, so I call his cell, holding my breath and crossing my fingers as it rings. I'm not sure what I'm hoping for, honestly. It won't exactly make things any better if he answers but is still angry.

My heart sinks when his voicemail message rings out in my ear. Even if the shop is busy, he would make time to answer if he felt like speaking to me. No, he would rather ignore my calls. I'm grinding my molars by the time a beep indicates the beginning of my message.

But when I open my mouth, my throat is too tight to allow an apology or anything else to come out. Flustered, I end the call without saying a word, then slap my palm against my forehead out of irritation with myself. This doesn't have to be rocket science, but I am completely clueless over what to do next. Somehow, I have to make things right. I need him to meet me halfway, however.

I text him, instead, chewing my lip as my thumbs fly over the screen. **I'm sorry. Really, I am. I would like to talk to you when you're ready. At least give me the chance to explain myself. That's all I ask.**

Granted, I'm a little annoyed when I send the message. He's upset, and I get it, but he's normally the first person to want to make peace. He doesn't normally make me jump through hoops like this.

It's only because he cares. I sigh wearily as I start the car, deciding to head to Mom's and get the rest I desperately need if there's any hope of fixing not only my personal life but the mystery surrounding Alyssa.

31

KILLER

Today, we're going on a little road trip. I do enjoy the opportunity to leave Broken Hill every once in a while.

So industrious, my Alexis. It surprised me to find her car in front of her mother's house for so much of the day yesterday. Surprise turned to concern when hours passed without her leaving. I worried she was ill, that she's pushed herself beyond the point of exhaustion thanks to her determination to find me. I suppose even she has to take time to sleep now and again. She can't always fight to save the entire world.

Today, though, she seems like her normal self except for one thing, avoiding her boyfriend's bookstore. Interesting, but not necessarily indicative of a deeper issue.

Once I realize where we're headed after following her for the better part of an hour, sheer delight makes my skin tingle. It isn't often I'm tickled by the actions of another, but then this is Alexis. She always finds ways to surprise me. She's going to the prison. She's going to talk to Russell Duffy, the man serving time for the murder of her sweet, precious sister.

I smile to myself, tapping my fingers against the wheel in time with the oldies playing on the radio. I prefer older music. Today's music has no heart and all sounds the same. Every genre has been watered down to the point where it all sounds like pop. Even the few singer songwriters out there are generic hacks.

When I heard they'd arrested a man in connection with Madeline's case, I admit I laughed myself sick. To think, I didn't even frame the guy. He simply happened to be the man the police decided was responsible. What was I going to do, tell them they were wrong? Turn myself in, ask him to forgive me? As time went on and it became clear even the loser's attorneys didn't believe his innocence, I could breathe easier. I mean, here I am, the picture of an innocent man. In my everyday life, I go out of my way not to be noticed. Another anonymous face in the crowd.

Not like Russell, who may as well have a sign around his neck that read *Guilty*. Of what? Virtually anything. Who would trust a known criminal? A drug dealer, a user, a thief?

If anything, I'm sort of a hero. I helped get a guilty man off the streets. Thanks to me, he couldn't commit any more robberies. No more selling drugs that could very well destroy lives. No more being a blight on society.

Many is the time I've thanked him silently for being in the right place at the right time at least as far as I'm concerned. He made it possible for me to continue my work, and my work is the most important thing in my life. Everything revolves around it. Nothing can get in its way. He made that possible. I even thought about him the first few years after Madeline left my presence, on the anniversary of our meeting. Thinking about him, about an innocent serving time for my behavior, warmed my heart twice as much.

And Alexis wants to see him. I wonder what else she could possibly have to say, since she's been there before. No doubt he swore his innocence, but I've wondered what else he shared. There have been times since that visit when my curiosity almost became too much to handle. It was almost enough to make me introduce myself to Alexis and ask her. That's the one thing about this situation that frustrates me the most. Having to speculate, to guess, to wonder.

One day soon, I will ask her to tell me every word they exchanged. I want to savor it like a fine wine or an exquisite meal. I want to know what he's been through all these years I've walked free.

What a shame I can't visit him myself, but even I know that would be too much of a risk. I haven't gotten this far without being arrested due to carelessness.

What I wouldn't give to know what she's thinking. Why a second visit? Does she think he'll give her some new information? Surely, she can't believe he has anything to do with the note I couldn't help but leave on her car. I'm going to look back on that with great fondness for a long time. Watching her chase her tail, observing from afar as she raced to that drugstore. She picked up every crumb I left – greedily, hungrily.

"Just wait and see what happens the next time I decide to reach out," I murmur. It takes all of my self-control not to indulge in fantasy here and now, as I drive. What matters more at the moment is keeping my distance so she doesn't notice me

Once we reach the prison and I fall back to wait for her, I'll have plenty of time to indulge my imagination.

32

ALEXIS

The man who takes a seat across from me has the same friendly, warm eyes as before. The same close-cropped hair, the same inquisitive smile. "Alexis. I didn't imagine I would ever see you again." It's entirely too bizarre, the way Russell smiles at me when he sits down on the other side of the plexiglass between us. Like I'm an old friend. Like my visit is something noteworthy.

Maybe I'm his only visitor. It's not like we don't have a connection. I only wish it didn't have to be such a dark, painful one.

He waits patiently enough while I fight to find the words to explain myself. Eventually, clears his throat before offering a gentle prompt. "What brings you here?"

The funny thing is, now that I'm here, it seems silly. I have no actual evidence to give him, and it would be wrong to offer a shred of hope without that. "I wanted to tell you about a development. It might lead to something great for you."

He tips his head to the side, eyes narrowing. "What is it?"

"Someone left a note on my car. It was threatening in nature. It said they knew I was searching for them, and there's only one person I'm searching for."

He still looks confused. "Who are you searching for?"

Now I feel downright idiotic for coming. I guess I expected him to make the connection right away. "Maddie's killer," I murmur, keenly aware of the visitors on either side of the dividers to my left and right. "I've been searching for him, whoever he is. Only it turns out he's aware of that – according to the message he left, anyway."

"Oh. I see. That's got to be nerve-wracking, right? That means he's in the area. And he knows who you are. I hope you're being careful," he says, frowning.

"As careful as I can be. I imagined you would be … "

"Happy?" he guesses before chuckling softly, the way someone does when they wish they could pat somebody on the head and tell them what an idiot they are. That's how it seems, anyway. "I would never be happy to hear someone is stalking you. I hope you don't think I would be."

This is turning into a disaster, the two of us on completely different pages. "No, that's not what I mean at all. It's a sign that whoever did this is still out there, and close enough that I could find him. That should be great news for you. It could get you out of here."

"It wouldn't be that easy, but I guess you would know that." Again, he looks sympathetic. Like I'm the one in prison for a crime I didn't commit. "Someone could confess, but there would still need to be evidence linking them to the crime. Otherwise, any random person on the street could overturn a conviction on a whim. Not that I'm trying to tell you about your business," he quickly adds. "But I did more than my share of research when I first got in here. I ran the gamut. What if someone confessed, what if a similar crime took place and it was obvious the same person committed both? Would that be enough to get my conviction overturned? The answer was always no. They would need solid evidence to back up a confession."

I know that. Of course I do. The fact that it takes an inmate to explain it to me doesn't provide much satisfaction as I sit back in my chair, increasingly miserable. "I guess I needed something positive to come out of the situation. If this person is determined to antagonize me, fine, so long as it means you getting out and having your conviction cleared from your record."

"That means a lot," he assures me. "To tell you the truth, life is not all bad in here. I told you before, during your first visit."

"I know, you studied and bettered yourself." But to what end? What does it matter if he's going to spend the rest of his life here?

His eyes light up and he leans in like he's excited. "Your first visit inspired me. I decided to go for my master's degree."

"Oh, that's great. In Literature?"

He shakes his head and a slow smile begins to stir the corners of his mouth. "Counseling and psychology. I want to help people the way you do."

At first, I'm too overwhelmed to speak. When I find my voice, it's soft, shaky. "I'm flattered."

"There are so many guys in here who need guidance," he tells me. I hear the excitement in his voice. He sounds determined, too. A man who's found his purpose. "I want them to see there's a better way. You can't spend all your time in here feeling resentful or wishing things were different. It can be a positive experience if you only try to look at it from a different perspective. It's one thing to hear that from, you know, the prison doctor or what have you. But to hear it from a fellow inmate? I feel like that would mean a lot more."

"Oh, I have no doubt." He's genuinely, wholeheartedly invested in this, and I wouldn't dare take it away from him. But doesn't he want to get out?

"I feel like I finally found my purpose," he continues. "If this is what I'm meant to do, then it means all of this happened for a reason. I don't mean just getting my life cleaned up. I get to pass that on. Pay it forward. You know how many guys get out of prison and end up right back where they came from, right?"

"I'm aware of the statistics, of course."

"If I can help just one guy get out of here and start down a better path, that's enough for me."

His excitement and determination are overwhelming. It's almost enough to make me wish I hadn't assumed how my news would make him feel. "I am so glad for you, I really am. To see you turn this into something positive and a way to give back is inspiring."

"It's all thanks to you. Really. I wouldn't have enrolled in courses to continue my studies if it hadn't been for your visit. Thank you for that."

"You're welcome." This is bordering on the absurd, at least from where I'm sitting. I expected him to pepper me with questions about the case. What it means now that I got that note, what to expect, what to hope for. "Can I ask you something, though? If I ended up catching the real killer, and if there were proof tying him to Maddie, wouldn't you be happy?"

His brows draw together before he releases a tiny sigh. "This might not be easy for you to understand, because you've never been on this side of the glass. But once enough time passes, you lose hope. You can either wallow in that or you can find a purpose. A meaning behind it. I lost that hope a long time ago. To tell you the truth, I'm not sure it isn't a waste of time and energy. I wouldn't want to entertain the idea for too long, because that would be the same as planting the seed of something I don't want to grow into a thornbush. Does that make any sense?"

"You don't want to get your hopes up, in other words."

"Something like that. Of course, I would like to see your sister's killer brought to justice. But even then, I would be happier for you and your parents getting the closure you deserve."

I don't know what to say. Nothing about this visit has gone the way I expected. I'm untethered, unsure of myself. "Thank you for that," I somehow manage while my mind swirls with questions and self-recrimination. I shouldn't have assumed he'd be thrilled.

"Don't worry about me," he insists. "I wouldn't say this is the happiest way any man's life could turn out, but it's probably the best mine could have. At least some small bit of good came out of all that tragedy. I understand you might not feel quite that way," he adds with a self-deprecating chuckle. "But rest assured, that's how I see it."

I'm glad one of us does.

33

ALEXIS

"At least you can tell yourself he's not suffering." Captain Felch looks sympathetic when he takes a seat at his desk once I've finished telling him the story of my visit yesterday. "It's remarkable, the fact that the experience didn't harden him."

"I know. If anything, it changed him into a much better man than the one he described during my first visit."

"The time he's spent inside turned him around. There's no need to feel guilty over him being in there. He might not be alive today, otherwise." He raises an eyebrow, looking me over before frowning. "You still seem troubled."

"Because I am troubled," I finally have to admit, though I'm sure it's not much of a mystery. "There's this feeling inside of me. I need to make sure he gets justice. Not only justice for us."

"That's not up to you." He wears a sad, knowing grin as he shakes his head. "There you go again. Trying to take care of everyone."

"What can I say?" I shrug, more than a little self-conscious. "It's a habit."

"You can't be so hard on yourself. And you know the old saying about leading a horse to water. You can't make Russell want what you think he should want."

"I know. But I don't have to like it."

"It isn't your fault he ended up where he did. A lot of people played a part in that, but you weren't one of them."

"I know that, too."

Leaning back in his chair, he smirks. "So that's what you did when you were supposed to be taking it easy yesterday."

"Hey, I took it easy after I left Alyssa at the hospital the other day. Yesterday, I felt rested up, so I took a drive." *It isn't like I had the option of seeing Mitch.* I'm still irked at the way he interfered in my personal life, but I don't want to start an argument.

"I knew better than to think you would stay home, anyway."

"What did I miss around here?" I ask, sipping my coffee. If the captain took notice of the different cups this morning, he hasn't said anything. I have no doubt he noticed. You don't become a captain without possessing a sharp eye for detail.

The fact is, I couldn't bring myself to visit Mitch's shop today. For one thing, he still hasn't responded to my text. That's beyond unusual for him, and the longer he stays silent, the greater the dread in my heart. I don't want to imagine life without him. Maybe I could get through it if we hadn't reconnected. The Alexis who first returned to Broken Hill thought she was fine with life as it was. She dreaded coming back here, back to the place where there had been so much pain and loss.

But this trip brought me many gifts. Reconnecting with my parents. Starting fresh with Mitch. It would be beyond cruel if I had to learn to live without him all over again.

He shrugs. "We're still waiting on a report from the lab. They've scoured Alyssa's clothes for any DNA, and I suppose it will take time to find a match — if there is one to be found," he points out. "If these kidnappers were new to the game, so to speak, there might not be a sample on file for them."

Something tells me that's exactly how this is going to pan out. The people who kidnapped her were completely new to kidnapping and trafficking, or else they would have sold her off long before she escaped. They wouldn't have made it so easy for her to escape, either – she would have been tied up, restrained somehow.

And that is if she were truly kidnapped. I'm not in the mood to have a debate about it, which is why I hold my tongue rather than get into it again with the captain. "I guess they'll release her soon from the hospital," I muse.

"I called over there last night. They said she should be free to go home today or tomorrow at the latest."

"I hope she and Connor manage to make it work now."

"I agree, if only for the sake of the children." He strokes his jaw thoughtfully with one hand while reaching for his coffee with the other. I notice the way he studies the cup before adding, "If their foundations are strong enough, they should be able to make it through this."

Now I wonder who he's talking about, the Lawrences, or me and Mitch. Right away, my pride rears up, threatening to make me say something stupid. I settle for chuckling before offering a shrug. "Who's to say? Sometimes it doesn't work out."

"Sometimes it doesn't," he agrees. "Normally, that comes from different values, different views on life. Fundamental differences, the sort of things you can't gloss over and pretend they don't exist. Other times, it's only a matter of compromise."

"Sure it is." He thinks he's slick – or maybe he doesn't. Maybe he knows exactly how heavy handed he is.

The phone call that interrupts us couldn't have come at a better time. Things are starting to get a little too personal for comfort, and before long I might have to point out how much trouble he's caused me. "Yes?" he murmurs once he answers. His eyes light up before they meet mine. "You did? In the area, you said?"

I scoot to the edge of my seat, my heart beating faster than ever. He scribbles down a few lines, nodding and murmuring. "That's great. Thank you."

The second he hangs up his desk phone, I practically jump across the desk. "I'm going to explode if you don't tell me what that was all about."

"That was about a DNA match obtained using hair taken from Alyssa's clothing. They must have worked around the clock to get it."

He's driving me insane, dragging his feet like this. "So?"

"The DNA found on Alyssa's clothes matches that of an ex-felon who lives outside Broken Hill, maybe twenty minutes beyond town limits." He reads the name off his notepad. "Gregory Morgandodder."

I pull out my phone and have him spell the name for me. While the captain types furiously on his laptop, I look up Gregory's Facebook profile. It shows me a man who according to his birthdate is thirty-five. He's handsome in a sharp, dangerous sort of way. His dark eyes are narrowed in a threatening stare in photos where he carries a guitar and looks like he's ready to beat somebody with it. The whole thing screams *I'm a moody musician*.

"I have a confirmation on his address," Captain Felch tells me, his voice ringing with excitement. "Feel like taking a ride?"

Nothing could stop me.

———

GREGORY LIVES in a rental outside town, the way the captain described. It's rather run down, but several of the houses on the block seem well cared for. There are snowmen on a couple of the lawns, sleds strewn around by happy kids.

There's no such happiness at Gregory's, where it doesn't look like he's picked up a shovel yet this season. The snow has merely melted and frozen until his front walk has essentially turned into a treacherous sheet of solid ice. It's easier for us to cut across the lawn, where there's at least a little more traction.

I notice the way the curtains shift at the windows of the house next door. What sort of neighbor is Gregory? Has he had any unwilling guests lately? Does he make a habit of this?

Captain Felch knocks on the door with me behind him and a pair of officers behind me. We're ready to defend ourselves if need be, all of us armed, though nothing in Gregory's record points to him being violent. His charges pertain to petty theft and possession. Even so, finding cops at the front door days after the woman he kidnapped escaped might inspire panic.

One thing I notice, the absence of a garage. There isn't a house with a garage on the block. All right, so maybe Alyssa wasn't held here, but Gregory paid her a visit. Maybe she was unconscious at the time and somehow, his hair got on her clothes.

Or maybe my gut is right and she made the whole thing up. I can hardly wait to hear his explanation.

The front door opens to reveal the man whose Facebook profile I reviewed earlier. One thing is for sure, those pictures are several years old. The man in front of us has crow's feet at the corners of his eyes, and a few touches of gray in his black hair. "What is this about?" he asks, his narrowed gaze bouncing from one of us to the other. His eyes are bloodshot, unfocused, and he scrubs a hand over the top of his head before yawning.

"Gregory Morgandodder?" Captain Felch asks.

"That's me." He still doesn't look like he appreciates the seriousness of the situation he's in.

He will soon enough. "We're going to need you to come in and answer some questions at the Broken Hill Police Station."

34

ALEXIS

I can smell the beer on his breath from the other side of the table. When we picked him up, it was barely 8:30 in the morning, and already he's buzzed – at least. "I really don't understand what this is about." He finishes gulping down the cup of coffee I brought him before offering a brief smile which I can imagine has charmed plenty of women. "Thanks. Sorry, I need to sober up a little bit."

"Are you in the habit of drinking this early in the morning?"

His head snaps back a little, and I can't tell if he's offended or confused. "I wasn't drinking this morning."

"With all due respect, you only finished telling me you need to sober up. Is that because you haven't been drinking?"

"Not this morning," he explains, even chuckling a little. "I was out late last night. I tend bar. I worked until close, then went out with some friends afterward. I didn't get in until almost five."

Pushing his floppy hair back with one hand, he shrugs. "I guess it was this morning, depending on how you look at it."

That makes sense, if it's true. "So that's what you do for a living? Tend bar?"

"That's it, and I pull in a little bit of extra here and there with my band." There's pride in his voice.

"Do you perform often?"

"Now and then." He folds his arms over his flat stomach, and I notice a Def Leppard t-shirt under his partially zipped hoodie. "Now that you know me a little better, why don't you tell me why I'm here? I'm answering your questions. You can answer mine."

"Fair enough." I fold my hands on the table, squaring my shoulders, getting into interrogation mode. If anything, I would rather cut to the chase. It isn't easy, affecting a friendly, personable air in front of a suspect who might be involved in a woman's kidnapping. "Your DNA has been linked to a crime scene."

Got him. His eyes nearly fall out of his head, and after a brief moment of complete shock, his Adam's apple bobs. "My DNA?"

"Yes." I check my notes to confirm. "It was extracted from hair left behind on the clothing of a woman who was kidnapped and held hostage. She recently escaped captivity."

His mouth moves in silent protest while his eyes dart back and forth like he's trying to piece this together. "I don't get it. How is that possible?"

"That's why you're here. For us to discuss how that's possible."

"I didn't kidnap anybody." He's going to strain his neck if he keeps shaking his head this hard. "No way."

"That's not the story she tells."

"She. Who is she? Who are we talking about? This has to be some kind of misunderstanding. Maybe somebody I hooked up with or somebody I gave a ride home to. I do that sometimes, when there's somebody at the bar who can't get an Uber and is too drunk to get home on their own." His eyes flash with hope and his voice rises in pitch. "That has to be it. I've never hurt anybody."

"You mean to tell me if I mention the name Alyssa Lawrence, it means nothing to you?"

His mouth falls open before he leans in. "Alyssa? She was kidnapped?"

Just like that, he turned the tables. One thing I can't do is show him how surprised I am at his reaction. "You recognize the name?" I ask.

"Sure. But nobody kidnapped her. She wasn't kidnapped." He shakes his head adamantly.

I've sort of suspected as much, but for him to be so sure? I sip my own coffee, stalling for time, deciding how to counter. Here I was, imagining he would deny ever knowing anyone of that name, yet the opposite has happened. Not only does he know her, but he's completely certain she wasn't kidnapped. If he's surprised or confused, it's because he's sure he knows otherwise.

"Let me get this straight," I begin, speaking slowly, feeling like a pilot building the plane while it's in midair. "You not only know Alyssa Lawrence, but you are certain she wasn't kidnapped."

"That's right."

"She says she was kidnapped and held hostage. How do you explain the way your stories contradict each other?"

"I don't have the first idea." Any hint of worry for himself has dissolved like cotton candy in the rain. It's almost like we're in this together, trying to figure out a problem while on the same team. He folds his arms on the table, tipping his head to the side and frowning. "What else did she tell you?"

"Let's backtrack a little," I suggest as gently as I can. Like I'm going to share vital details of the case because he asked nicely. "You know Alyssa Lawrence personally?"

He snorts before nodding. "Yeah, I know her personally."

"And what is the nature of your acquaintance?"

"Nature of our acquaintance?" He laughs gently, almost like he's sorry for me. "You mean how do we know each other? What's our history?"

I lift a shoulder. "Whatever works."

"She's my ex-girlfriend. We dated for about six months before she decided she wanted a guy with a steady career." He rolls his eyes, telling me how he feels about this.

It's not easy to hide my surprise. At times like this, an air of professionalism is more challenging than ever. "And when was the last time you saw her?"

"When she showed up at my front door."

My heart is ready to pound out of my chest, and my throat is so tight I can barely speak. Adrenaline is pumping through my veins, making it difficult to sit still. "And when was that? That she showed up at your front door, I mean."

"I remember the exact day. She showed up one afternoon out of nowhere, when we hadn't seen each other in years. It was raining a little and her hair was wet. She was a crying mess. She said I was the only person she could go to."

"Did she tell you what she was upset about?"

"Sure. She said it was because of her husband. How he was awful, and how she had to get away from him. She asked if she could stay with me, and I said yes."

35

ALEXIS

I'm reeling. It's not exactly professional to reveal my level of surprise at what Gregory has shared, but I can't help it. I had a feeling, didn't I? I knew there was something wrong with Alyssa's story. But this? Running to an ex-boyfriend, then claiming she was kidnapped? Who would go to such lengths?

Gregory sits in silence while I process this as quickly as I can. She made it up. She was lying.

Or was she? It could be he's making this up, too. I can't discount her simply because I don't quite believe her. I take another sip of coffee, then a deep breath to steady myself. "Let's start at the beginning. Exactly what happened? How did this start?"

"Just like I told you. She showed up at my house out of nowhere and was, like, hysterical, crying. She said her husband was terrible and she needed help."

"Did she specify how he was terrible?" I ask. "Did she supply any proof?"

He rubs the back of his neck, almost like he's searching his memory, frowning as he does it. "You know, I'm not sure. I was so surprised to see her, and you know, I wanted to help. I figured if she had to run away, there was a reason for it. Even if he wasn't really doing anything to hurt her."

"When you dated Alyssa, did she ever do anything like this? Running off out of nowhere, checking out of her own life?"

He shakes his head firmly. "And that's why I wanted to believe her. That's not the kind of person she is. She wouldn't walk away from her life."

I need to think. If she made this up, I would love nothing more than to nail her for wasting our resources. Let's not get started on how she abandoned her children – well, not exactly, they had their father. But at that age, a little one wants their mommy. "All right, so what happened next?"

"I told her she could crash with me for a while if she needed to."

"And she did?" He nods, and I make a note of it followed by a question mark. It seems that's all I have to go with so far. A bunch of question marks.

"Yeah, it was kind of weird, but she made sure I knew she didn't want to get in my way. I would go to work at night, and she would stay around the house, watching TV or whatever. She cleaned the place up a little bit for me, did my laundry. I picked her up a couple things when I was out one day so she'd have more clothes to wear than what she showed up in. Then we would just hang out together when I was home. It was sort of nice, like having a roommate."

There's nothing about his demeanor – tone of voice, body language, any of it – to give me a hint of him lying. If anything, he seems almost glad to be sharing the story. I suppose it all seemed very strange to him. It might be a relief to unload a little.

With that in mind, I relax my posture, resting my chin on my palm and tapping my pen against my notepad. "That's all that happened? You went to work, you came home, she was kind of a homemaker for you?"

I glance up from my notes in time to find him frowning. "Did I say something wrong?" I ask.

He shakes his head. "No, but … that's not all that happened."

"Did things get physical? Is that what you're trying to say?"

His face falls, and now he's shifting uncomfortably in the chair. Almost squirming. "We shouldn't have done it. I know that. She's still married, and I don't hook up with married women. But she wanted to have a little fun one night, so we sat around drinking on my night off and got way too drunk. You know, talking about the way things used to be, listening to music. And we ended up sleeping together."

"I see. Was that the only time?"

"Oh, yeah, I knew it was a mistake as soon as I sobered up. But she kept telling me it didn't matter, because her marriage was a joke anyway." If she knew about or even suspected Connor's affair with Meredith, I can imagine her feeling that way.

"Did she ever mention her husband's behavior?" I ask, curious. Was this all a way of getting revenge on him? Reminding him of everything he was squandering by playing fast and loose with his marriage vows?

Gregory only shrugs. "She never said anything specific. But I kind of got the idea that maybe he was screwing around on her. I didn't want to ask any questions that might hurt, so I didn't bother. Anyway, it was another couple of days before she left."

"And whose idea was that?"

"Hers. She said it was time to go home."

The way his brow creases tells me it wasn't as simple as that. There's nothing simple about this case. "When she decided it was time to leave …" I begin, carefully weighing my words. "What did she look like? What was her condition?"

His eyes light up and I know that was the right question. He leans in a little closer, even breathing a little faster. "That was the weirdest part. I already thought it was kind of strange that she was barely eating. I asked her about it, too. She would make food for me, but then she would barely eat anything herself. She would always wave it off, like it was no big deal. But then, before she was leaving, she asked me to…"

His voice dies, and he slumps a little. "It's so bizarre."

"What is?" I prompt gently.

"She…" He releases a silent, disbelieving laugh. "She wanted me to punch her in the face."

There's no smothering my reaction to that. After closing my open mouth and composing myself, I ask, "She specifically asked you to punch her?"

He nods, slowly, never breaking eye contact. "Like I said. Bizarre."

"And what did you say?"

"No!" he scoffs. "I said no. I wasn't going to hurt her. She even tried to pick a fight, tried to get me to push her around a little, but I wasn't going for it. So she did it herself."

"Did what?"

"She punched herself. Hard. While I was watching." He shakes his head and shivers a little. "Man, let me tell you. I was glad she was leaving when I saw her do that. She's completely messed up. I didn't need her around."

It's not easy, imagining a woman inflicting injury upon herself. The memory of her black eye is fresh. I don't think I could do it. "Did she ever tell you why she wanted you to do that?"

"I asked her! I was like, dude, what's wrong with you? She didn't just punch herself, either. She, like, rubbed her wrists really hard so they would be marked up. She flung herself against the wall. I thought I was gonna have to call the police, I really did. I was like, Alyssa, stop. Why would you do this to yourself? She said it was all so she could start a new career."

"What?" I whisper. "What kind of career could that possibly start?"

"Victim advocate. She wanted to become a speaker. An influencer." He makes air quotes around the word. "Like, if she could help people through experiences like the one she had, she would be famous."

"She admitted that to you." It isn't a question. It's more a statement born of absolute shock. The audacity. Not to mention the level of trust she must possess. Why in the world would she think anybody would accept that as a reasonable course of action?

"She always was kind of … off. Not in a way that she would ever hurt people or anything. But once she gets an idea in her head, that's it. You can't convince her she's wrong. And if you try to get in her way, she'll bulldoze right over you. it's funny," he muses with a chuckle. "I used to like that about her. That was one of the things that drew me to her, you know? But now?" He doesn't have to say another word. I understand what he means.

All that's left now is figuring out who is telling the truth. At the moment, my money is on the man sitting across from me, if only because Alyssa has set herself up as the party with something to prove. She still has to come up with a plausible explanation for how she escaped captivity. As far as I know, whenever anyone asks her, she claims shock or brain fog or fatigue. She has given us nothing to point us toward her captors, and the entire story of the events of her captivity is spotty at best.

I feel like I've been through a hurricane by the time I clear my throat. "Thank you for taking the time to tell me all of this. Depending upon what we find, we may need to bring you back in." Something tells me we won't need to. There's my gut, right on schedule.

I usher Gregory out of the interrogation room and one of the deputies who brought him in offers to drive him home. Captain Felch exits the door on the other side of the two-way glass. Our eyes meet and his mouth pulls into a tight, thin line. There's no question of what happens next.

It's time to bring Alyssa Lawrence in for questioning.

36

ALEXIS

"I'll watch along with Dr. Lawrence." Captain Felch looks as grim as he sounds while we observe the Lawrences interacting on the monitor. Connor keeps rubbing Alyssa's shoulders, and the smile she offers can only be described as brave. The little survivor, the heroine who immediately goes back to whatever she was doing on her phone after acknowledging her husband.

To think, I was so sure he had something to do with it. I don't doubt he's sorry now for all of his infidelity. He wants to make things right. To make her happy.

What a shame I'm about to get in the way of all of that. Then again, I'm not the person who faked their own kidnapping.

The captain comes with me, murmuring to Connor that he would like to see him outside while I speak with his wife. Connor and Alyssa exchange a look, but Alyssa nods. "Go ahead. I'll be fine."

On his way from the room, he makes sure to catch my eye. Words are unnecessary. I can read his thoughts as clearly as if they were typed across his face. His wife has already been through enough. He is ultra protective now. He'll never let anyone hurt his wife ever again. Not even himself.

Alyssa is still on her phone when we're alone and I take a seat. *Your ex-boyfriend sat in that chair earlier.* It might be worth blurting that out if only to gauge her reaction, which I can imagine would be one of shock and maybe horror. "You look pretty busy," I observe, nodding to her device.

"You wouldn't believe the messages I've been getting." Her cheeks are pink and her eyes shining as she holds out her phone, scrolling through her inbox so I can see the dozens upon dozens of direct messages sent through her Facebook account. "Complete strangers. They heard about my kidnapping and they want to offer support, or to talk about their own experiences. I want to make something positive out of this. Maybe I can help other people who have been through similar traumas."

"I bet you could make a career out of something like that."

"Oh, I don't know." She giggles softly and waves it off as if she hasn't already entertained that idea. "I mean, it would be nice. But I really just want to help people. I'm part of a club now, I guess. The sort of club nobody wants to belong to."

My goodness. She certainly spent her free time at Gregory's perfecting her lines, didn't she? What a shame she didn't spend more time coming up with a plausible kidnapping story. It takes real effort to maintain a pleasant expression. "I'm sure you're very busy and would rather be home, but there are a few things we want to get straight."

Finally she sets the phone aside. "Of course. Anything I can do to help."

What better way to get started than to jump right in? "We ran DNA tests on evidence found on your clothes."

Her eyelashes flutter. "I didn't know I had any evidence on my clothes."

"That's what the forensics team is good at. Finding what the rest of us would ordinarily miss. There were hairs on your clothes that didn't belong to you, so they were tested, and there was a hit on the DNA."

"Hit?" There's no way she's not understanding me, but I suppose she's hoping to plead ignorance and maybe come up with an excuse for all of this.

"Yes, there was a match in the database. An ex-convict."

"Who was it?" She sits at attention, her eyes wide. "Maybe this is how we catch them." She's not going to make it easy. I didn't expect her to.

"His name is Gregory Morgandodder."

She swallows hard but says nothing. There's practically smoke coming from her ears, though, and her jaw ticks. How is she going to explain her way out of this one?

"Do you recognize the name?" I ask, still keeping up the act. "It's sort of an uncommon one."

"I ..." Her tongue darts over her lips.

"Do you know him?" I murmur.

"Gregory ... What did you say the last name was?"

Enough of this. "Alyssa, you know what the last name is. And you know Gregory, and he's already told us everything."

All at once, her face goes red. "What do you mean, told you everything? There's nothing to tell! What, was he in here? Telling lies?" She snorts. It's sort of amazing the way she can flip from the saintly, innocent mother to the bitter, hostile woman before me.

"He told me you showed up at his front door unannounced, crying and telling him about how awful things are with your husband. He gave you a place to crash. Once you announced it was time to leave, you asked him to assault you so you would look injured."

"He's lying! Why would I ever do that?"

"I have an idea, but I would like you to tell me. Why would an ex-boyfriend make up a story like that?"

"Because … Because …" She looks around, breathing fast, skating on the edge of panic. "Because he's the one who did it! It might've been his van. He might have had those people take me for himself. Wouldn't it make sense if he owned the van that his hair would be in there somewhere? Isn't that possible?"

I'm not going to feed into her mania. My best course of action is to sit perfectly still, staring at her, waiting while she unravels her own plot. "Is that what happened, Alyssa?" I ask once she's gone silent aside from her gasps for breath.

"It has to be!"

"How did you escape? How did you make it out of there? How did you find your way to the gas station? Approximately how far away was it from the place where you were held? It's been days, and you've been unable to provide any information that might help us. Now, you're telling me everything Gregory reported is a lie. If it is, please, counter with the truth."

She swallows hard while the color drains from her face. I wait, calm and patient.

Finally, she lowers her head. "The idiot. He wasn't supposed to say anything," she murmurs.

And there it is. There's the final nail in the coffin. All of the glowing, positive things people have to say about her, and this is what it's come to. "In other words, he told the truth? Right down to the injuries you inflicted upon yourself?"

"All right, fine." All at once, she decides to switch tracks. That's typically what happens when a person knows they've hit a brick wall and need to course correct. "I wasn't actually kidnapped."

That's it. She doesn't offer an apology. She doesn't seem the least bit sorry or like she has the first clue what she's cost all of us. "Is that all you have to say?" I ask.

"Well, it's not like I did anything wrong. I went away. I came back. I didn't hurt anybody."

The fact that she can sit there and look me in the face and say these things without a hint of understanding baffles me. She honestly believes what she's saying. That just because nobody got hurt, this should all be glossed over. Life can go on. "You make it sound like you took a vacation, Mrs. Lawrence. What you did was really quite serious."

"But … I didn't hurt anybody …" To my surprise, her chin begins to quiver. "I didn't do anything wrong. I just wanted a story."

"Story?" I asked, confused.

"A platform." She sniffles pitifully. "Something to launch my brand."

If I didn't know better, I would swear I was on a prank show. The worst part is, she believes herself. She's sincere. "So you chose a fake kidnapping? And exactly how did you plan on parlaying that into a brand?"

"I wanted to be a speaker. Like I told you before. That was my plan. I wanted to help people."

"But you had no authentic experience to pull from. That's a great insult to people who've actually gone through the sort of ordeal you tried to fake. Trust me," I continue while her eyes widen and fill with genuine tears. "Once word got out about you, somebody on the internet would start digging. They would identify the inconsistencies in your story.

Heaven forbid you had already gained a following by the time that happened. They would turn on you in a heartbeat."

"That's not how it would've gone," she insists, her voice shaking with something far more intense than the crocodile tears she originally attempted. Now I see the Alyssa described by Gregory. Determined to the point of irrational behavior.

"I can tell you what's going to happen next." There's no pleasure in this, but I can't pretend I don't enjoy watching her face fall. "Since you misused the resources of the county, the state, and the FBI, you will be prosecuted to the fullest extent of the law and most likely fined to recoup our losses."

"Your losses?" she nearly shouts.

"We searched for you around the clock, Mrs. Lawrence, while you crashed with your ex-boyfriend. That's a lot of wasted manpower." After a brief moment spent observing her shell shocked expression, I stand. "Now, one of the department's deputies will take you to be fingerprinted and processed."

She's weeping by the time the door opens and a pair of officers enter the room, insisting weakly that this was all a misunderstanding. I can only watch with a heavy heart as I remember the two children who've now lost their mother a second time.

37

ALEXIS

I t isn't until I've left the interrogation room that I remember Alyssa didn't come in here alone.

"Dr. Lawrence!" I turn at the sound of Captain Felcher's sharp warning only to find Connor barreling toward me from the captain's office. He's red-faced, shaking, glaring at the back of his wife's head while she's led away.

"Hang on a second." I might be taking my life in my hands, but I place myself in his path, feinting left and right in response to him trying to get past me. I am not going to blame him for his emotional reaction, but that doesn't mean I can allow him to exacerbate things.

"Get out of my way," he growls.

"I can't do that." When he lunges like he's going to move through me if he has to, I lift my chin and look him in the eye. "Do I need to remind you that you're in the presence of an FBI agent? I would hate to leave those beautiful kids of yours with both of their parents behind bars."

That's what does it. He might not completely fold, but he certainly loses some of his fire. "She made it up," he whispers, trembling.

"I know. And I am sorry you had to witness her confession, truly. Come with me" He is still entirely too emotional and reactive to be left alone. I place a hand on his shoulder and steer him into the interrogation room his wife just left. He needs to cool down. I would hate to find out he was in an accident after leaving here because he was so worked up.

"I believed her. Why would I not? She's my wife!" His voice is loud enough to make me cringe, but I only stand with my back to the closed door while he paces, grunting, clenching his fists.

"I mean, what was she thinking?" he bellows while running both hands through his hair, and from where I stand it almost looks like he's pulling at it. He is completely losing control. My heart goes out to him, really. He was unfaithful, but what she did goes head and shoulders beyond a simple affair.

"Honestly, I don't understand any better than you do," I confess in a measured voice. I need him to calm down. It only occurs to me when he punches his open palm who he reminds me of at this moment, a grieving parent, feeling helpless and hopeless, raving about the fact that he was robbed of something. That his family was destroyed.

And I know from experience where that feeling can lead a man. The thought chills my blood. He's all his children have now.

"Maybe you should have a seat," I suggest, going to the table and pulling out a chair. "Really. I need you to sit down, and I need you to take a few deep breaths."

"That's easy for you to say. First, you're ready to arrest me. And now—"

"Dr. Lawrence, I was conducting an investigation. Believe me when I tell you I take no pleasure in any of this. I am very sorry, really I am." I point to the chair.

His glittering eyes meet mine and his lip curls in a snarl, but he does take the chair, dropping into it before leaning forward and holding his head in his hands. "What am I going to do? What do I tell the kids? Our family, our neighbors? Not to mention the money?"

Yes, I can imagine worrying about all of that. "This is going to sound trite," I offer, sitting on the edge of the table. I can't remember the last time I spoke to the family member of a criminal. Or a victim, for that matter. All of the professionalism falls away, and now we're only two people having a conversation. "But you can't think of everything all at once. You'll drive yourself out of your mind if you do. There's a reason the concept of taking things one day at a time exists. That's what you're going to need to do."

"That's easy for you to say. Your life didn't blow up in front of your face just now. I had to stand there with that Captain Felch guy and find out my wife ran off with some ex-boyfriend while I was losing my mind, going through being blamed for her disappearance. Worrying that she was dead. Trying to take care of the kids and maintain a happy face for their sake while I was dying inside. Very easy for you to tell me to take things one day at a time when you witnessed all of it from outside."

"I understand your feelings. I really do." When he snorts, I know it's time to break out the big guns. "Can I tell you something? This isn't something a lot of people know."

"Sure," he mutters without lifting his head. "Knock yourself out."

"When I was ten years old, someone murdered my sister."

His hands drop and his head lifts. His red rimmed eyes meet mine. "I'm sorry."

"It was here, in Broken Hill. She was fifteen. It took a month for her body to be discovered—but she had only been out there for a little while, meaning the killer kept her with him all that time." His features draw together when he winces. "I wouldn't normally tell you this, but as a person whose childhood was rocked by the worst thing imaginable, I need to remind you to keep those kids first and foremost in your mind. I know it sounds trite and obvious, but grief and anger can make a person do terrible things. Things they would never imagine under any other circumstances. In my case, my father shot the man who was convicted."

There it is. There's the recognition in his eyes. "Oh, I've heard of that. Out on the courthouse steps."

"People still talk about it to this day, almost twenty years later," I sigh. "I was left with my mother, who then had to bear the brunt of two tragedies. She lost her daughter, and she lost her husband once he went to prison. I know how it feels to lose one parent, then to essentially lose another to their pain. I would hate to see that happen to your children, Dr. Lawrence. I can't control what you say you do, and I can't follow you around and make sure you don't do anything rash. I can only ask you to keep them in mind. Keep my warning in mind. Can you do that for me?"

He draws a deep breath and sits up straighter. "I'll stay calm for their sake," he decides, his jaw tightening.

"I have your word on that?"

"Yes, Agent Forrest. You have my word on that." He stands, shakes out his hands, then offers what might be an apologetic glance. "I'm sorry. But thank you for talking to me. You didn't have to do it."

"You know how it is. You tell yourself you might be able to avoid somebody else going through what you went through, which makes it worth it."

He has a long road ahead of him, and I don't envy him one bit. His kids have a long road ahead of them, too. I'm glad they're too young now to understand the scandal that's about to erupt. Naturally, people are going to get wind of this–especially since, as Alyssa told me, she was already receiving messages from well-wishers and victims. No doubt that rush of goodwill is about to turn sour really fast.

38

ALEXIS

It's freezing out here, and I'm pretty sure my backside is permanently attached to the front steps of Mitch's house. A look at my phone tells me it's well past closing time at the store. He should be here any minute.

I'm starting to think I should have gone directly to the store rather than wait for him here, but the idea is to be alone with him. We need to hash things out, and we're not going to be able to do that effectively while in front of others.

I only wish I had imagined him keeping me waiting this long. I rub my arms briskly, shivering in the cold. The street is pleasant and inviting on a night like this, with many of the houses already lit from inside. There is nothing like the sight of what look like warm, happy homes when you're fairly sure your body is turning to ice. Wouldn't it be my luck if

Mitch decided to head over to The Tipsy Traveler or one of the other Main Street pubs tonight of all nights?

Before I can think better of the whole idea and leave with my tail between my legs, his familiar car turns the corner and rolls my way. If Mitch is dismayed to find me sitting in front of his house, he doesn't show it, merely parking in front of the house and stepping out without stalling. But he doesn't climb the stairs at first. He settles for folding his arms and looking up at me, raising his eyebrows. "What brings you here?" he asks.

It's startling, what the sound of his voice does to me. I haven't heard it in days, and now the tension I wasn't aware existed in my chest and my shoulders melts away. What a shame that warmth won't melt the cold stiffening the rest of me. "I wanted to see you."

"You see me." He spread his arms wide. "Anything else?"

"Sure." There goes my frustration, right on schedule. I want to accuse him of being unfair, to stomp my feet and insist I did nothing to deserve this. That's not going to work this time. "I want to apologize. I want us to work through this and get beyond it."

He shoves his hands into the pockets of his coat, scuffing a patch of icy snow with the toe of his shoe. "What are you sorry for?"

At the moment, I'm sorry I ever started this, because he won't be happy until I freeze to death. "I'm sorry I isolated myself from you. I told myself it was to keep you from worrying about me, but I understand now that it pushed you away. That's the last thing I want. I don't want you away from me. I want you closer to me. I want us to be together more than anything."

Pursing his lips, he takes one step closer to the house. Another. My heart swells a little more with every step he takes. "So you're going to stop keeping secrets about your work?"

"Yes. I will"

Another step. "And when something potentially dangerous happens, you're going to tell me about it so I can help you through it?"

"So long as you don't make me feel like I have to report to you at the end of every workday."

"I'll do my best," he murmurs with a smirk before quickly crossing the rest of the space left between us, hauling me to my feet and engulfing me in a bear hug that lights me up inside.

"Does this mean I'm forgiven?" I ask, my voice muffled against his shoulder.

"You're forgiven. You've been forgiven for a few days." He presses a firm kiss against my forehead before releasing a sigh. "I was feeling stubborn and didn't want to be the first one to break down."

"Oh, now you tell me." I pull back, rolling my eyes, but all that does is make him hold me closer. I have to laugh as I melt into his embrace.

"This is going to be the world's shortest lived romance unless we get inside," he announces, shivering a little before pulling his keys from his pocket and unlocking the front door. My relief is profound. I'm back where I belong.

It's clear he feels the same way, removing his coat before removing mine, then wrapping me in his embrace once again. "I've missed you."

"I've missed you, too," I murmur, breathing deep of his familiar scent, letting it soak into my bones. A reminder that I'm back where I belong.

He pulls back far enough to capture my lips with his and I accept his kiss happily, even greedily. One after another, I drink them in until it suddenly feels a little too warm in the house. My blood is pumping and my breath is a little short by the time we come up for air. "I've missed that, too," he growls, squeezing me a little tighter before letting go. "Are you hungry?"

"Very." Not entirely for food, but I suppose that can come first. My heart is brimming over with happiness as I follow him to the kitchen, where he heats up half a pan of lasagna for us along with a loaf of bread from the freezer.

We wait for the food, snacking on cheese and crackers and catching each other up on what we both missed. Camille is doing well, back on her old schedule at the store and feeling stronger all the time. Unlike Alyssa Lawrence, she was a true victim of kidnapping, someone who was lucky to escape with her life. When I think of her, I can only feel anger toward Alyssa. I'm sure people like Camille are exactly the sort of people she was looking to target with her survivor story.

And when I tell Mitch about it, it's clear we're thinking along the same lines. Not that I'm surprised. "She honestly thought she was going to get away with it?" he asks as disgust washes over his face. "I can't believe it. I've never heard anything like it."

"She thought it would be that simple," I explain with a shrug. "I don't pretend to understand, even with a PhD. Obviously, she got caught up in the idea of being a famous influencer, an influential speaker, whatever. And she concocted a harebrained scheme she couldn't be bothered to fully plan out. As if we would take her word for it without so much as wondering how she escaped."

"I'm sure she figured everybody would be so happy to see her, they wouldn't ask questions."

"I guess the joke is on her, though I doubt she thinks it's very funny."

It isn't until we've sat down with our dinner that Mitch addresses the elephant in the room, the one thing we haven't discussed yet. "I imagine if you received any new messages, you would've told me about it by now." He glances up from his lasagna, arching an eyebrow.

"No, you're right. I would've told you by now."

"I imagine one message was enough."

My teeth grind together at the thought. "More than enough. It irks me worse than I can explain, knowing we fell for his game so easily. I can't tell you how it bothers me."

"He wanted you to chase your tail – but he also wants you to feel this way. He wants you to start doubting yourself. He wants you to look over your shoulder and wonder if he's somewhere nearby. Don't give him that power."

I have to laugh at how simply he puts it. "I really have missed you," I tell him, chuckling at myself. "You always know what to say."

"Is that all I'm good for?" he asks, arching an eyebrow. "That's all you missed about me?"

"No, that's not all." I lean across the table to deliver a soft, lingering kiss. He tastes like tomato sauce and garlic and I don't think anything has ever tasted better. Ending the kiss, I murmur, "I also missed your bread."

"Clearly, that's what I was referring to," he retorts, and we share a laugh before sharing another kiss that turns into another, then another after that. Pretty soon we've both forgotten the rest of what's left on our plates, going straight to dessert. It just so happens that tonight, dessert is being served in the bedroom.

39

ALEXIS

"D o me a favor?" Mitch's breath tickles my ear when he draws me close and whispers in the darkness. "Let's pretend the rest of the world doesn't exist today."

It sounds like heaven. "You have no idea how much I would like to do that."

He snuggles closer and murmurs, "I doubt it. I have a pretty good idea myself. I can take the day off. Do you have anywhere you absolutely need to be?"

Now that Alyssa's case is wrapped up, I don't. "Well, I had planned on doing a little more digging into Maddie," I admit.

I roll over to face him, running a hand over his scruffy cheek. I've seen his face so many times I know it by heart even in the darkness of predawn. "Last night was amazing, but I still have to be ready in case something happens and they want to transfer me elsewhere. You know that, right?"

"I know it. But nobody has called you back to Boston yet." There's hope in his voice before he kisses the palm of my hand. "And even if they do call you back, that's not so terribly far. I could come down one weekend, you could come up the next. We would work something out."

"Am I really worth the effort?"

His head snaps back, and I can understand why. I never expected to blurt that question out. Now that it's there, I may as well stand behind it. "With everything I've put you through," I point out, "I can't imagine why you'd want to jump through all those hoops to keep us together."

"That's not how I see it at all." He pulls me close, until I can hear his heart beating under my ear. "I see it as doing what we have to do to make it work. I want to make it work. You're worth driving down to Boston every other weekend, or whatever we decide to do. I would gladly put the miles on the car if it meant being with you. We'll find a way."

He's right. He makes it sound so simple, but maybe it is. Maybe I have myself all twisted up for no reason. If he believes we can make this work, that's enough for me. "Do me a favor and bring baked goods with you if and when that happens."

"As if I wouldn't." Though neither of us has brushed our teeth yet, that doesn't stop us from sharing more than a few kisses which are about to turn into some more when my phone rings.

He groans but releases me. "Must be serious at this time of day," he points out, nodding toward the window where gray light has begun to filter through. That doesn't exactly thrill me, considering the much more pleasant way my morning was starting to go.

It's a Virginia number, and my pulse takes off like a horse right out of the gate before I answer. "Alexis Forrest."

"This is Agent Green at the field office in Virginia," the man on the other end announces in a voice heavy with fatigue. "Sorry it took so long to process that note you FedExed over to us, but it looks like we finally found something."

I sit up, gasping softly and looking at Mitch. "I'll put on the coffee," he offers, getting out of bed and pulling on jeans and a sweater before heading out of the room.

While he does, I ask, "And? What did you find?"

"Half a print. It's very small, but we were able to find a match based on what was left behind. It belongs to a man by the name of Tyler Mahoney."

I can barely breathe. A name. Still, I have to take my time rather than jump into conclusions the way I did at first. "Are we sure that's not somebody from around here? Maybe the kid working at the store?"

"Not unless the kid who worked at the store also worked as a lifeguard at a country club on Martha's Vineyard back in the 1990s."

I'm going to assume the kid I spoke to was not of such an age back in the nineties. I don't even think he was born yet. "And you're sure of this?"

"Apparently, this place was very protective of its members and their children. The club made sure to print all of their employees before bringing them on, checking them against local records to make sure they weren't making a mistake."

This is it. This is what I needed. Tyler Mahoney. The name is burned into my brain by the time I thank the agent and end the call, trembling with excitement as I pull my clothes on, prepared to share the good news with Mitch.

Except he's not in the kitchen once I reach the first floor. "Mitch? Where did you go?" I call out, and there's nothing to answer me but silence. My excitement pops like a balloon and dread takes its place—that is, until I notice the front door is partly open. I head toward it, peering outside, sighing with relief when I find Mitch standing next to his car.

That is, until I notice the words that have been scrawled on his windshield.

Forgetting the cold, I go out without my coat on, running down the front steps and joining Mitch on the sidewalk. His tires have been slashed, I notice now, but it's the red letters on the windshield that hold my attention.

Paint? Marker? Ink? I can't tell. I can only read the message and struggle to understand its meaning while Mitch wraps an arm around my shoulders.

I'm coming for you, Alexis. But first, your mom.

THANK for you reading Forest of Secrets. Can't wait to find out what happens to Alexis next? **Grab Forest of Lies now!**

Forensic psychologist and FBI agent Alexis Forrest returns in her most chilling case yet. Set against the backdrop of Broken Hill, the small New England town where she grew up, she now faces her darkest challenge: a fourteen-year-old boy doesn't show up to school after spending the night with his father and stepmother.

Meanwhile, Alexis receives a sinister note threatening her and her family from the serial killer who took her sister's life.

Together with her old flame and partner Mitch, a bookstore and coffee shop owner, Alexis embarks on a race against time to protect her loved ones and capture the predator who always seems to be one step ahead.

Amidst the chaos, Alexis grapples with haunting questions: Is the missing boy just a teenage runaway or a victim of the serial killer who haunts this area?

When a fire consumes her father's mobile home, Alexis finds herself in the path of the murderer who's been the source of her nightmares since she was a teen.

The only difference is that now she knows his name.

1-click Forest of Lies now!

———

IF YOU ENJOYED THIS BOOK, please don't forget to leave a review on Amazon and Goodreads! Reviews help me find new readers.

If you have any issues with anything in the book or find any typos, please email me at Kate@ kategable.com. Thank you so much for reading!

ALSO CHECK out my other bestselling and 3 time Silver Falchion award winning series, **Girl Missing.**

When her 13-year-old sister vanishes on her way back from a friend's house, Detective Kaitlyn Carr must confront demons from her own past in order to bring her sister home.

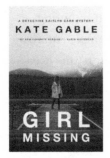

The small mountain town of Big Bear Lake is only three hours away but a world away from her life in Los Angeles. It's the place she grew up and the place that's plagued her with lies, death and secrets.

As Kaitlyn digs deeper into the murder that she is investigating and her sister's disappearance, she finds out that appearances are misleading and few things are what they seem.

A murderer is lurking in the shadows and the more of the mystery that Kaitlyn unspools the closer she gets to danger herself.

Can Kaitlyn find the killer and solve the mystery of her sister's disappearance before it's too late?

What happens when someone else is taken?

1-click Girl Missing now!

ABOUT KATE GABLE

Kate Gable loves a good mystery that is full of suspense. She grew up devouring psychological thrillers and crime novels as well as movies, tv shows and true crime.

Her favorite stories are the ones that are centered on families with lots of secrets and lies as well as many twists and turns. Her novels have elements of psychological suspense, thriller, mystery and romance.

Kate Gable lives near Palm Springs, CA with her husband, son, a dog and a cat. She has spent more than twenty years in Southern California and finds inspiration from its cities, canyons, deserts, and small mountain towns.

She graduated from University of Southern California with a Bachelor's degree in Mathematics. After pursuing graduate studies in mathematics, she switched gears and got her MA in Creative Writing and English from Western New Mexico University and her PhD in Education from Old Dominion University.

Writing has always been her passion and obsession. Kate is also a USA Today Bestselling author of romantic suspense under another pen name.

Write her here:

Kate@kategable.com

Check out her books here:

www.kategable.com

Sign up for my newsletter:
https://www.subscribepage.com/kategableviplist

Join my Facebook Group:
https://www.facebook.com/groups/
833851020557518

Bonus Points: Follow me on BookBub and Goodreads!

https://www.bookbub.com/authors/kate-gable

https://www.goodreads.com/author/show/21534224.
Kate_Gable

ALSO BY KATE GABLE

Missing Lives
Girl in the Lake

Made in United States
North Haven, CT
30 April 2024

51954084R00200